EXIT STRATEGY

a novel

JULIE FINIGAN MORRIS

authorHOUSE®

AuthorHouse™
1663 Liberty Drive
Bloomington, IN 47403
www.authorhouse.com
Phone: 1 (800) 839-8640

Cover illustration: Shiga toxin type 2 (Stx2) from Escherichia coli O157-H7 By: Fvasconcellos
Author's photograph: Elaine Patarini

Published by AuthorHouse 03/21/2017

ISBN: 978-1-5246-7000-9 (sc)
ISBN: 978-1-5246-6999-7 (hc)
ISBN: 978-1-5246-6998-0 (e)

Library of Congress Control Number: 2017901464

Print information available on the last page.

This book is printed on acid-free paper.

A crisis is a terrible thing to waste.

—Paul Romer

For Joe.

CONTENTS

Part II - Dreamers

Part III - Farmers

PART I

Thought Leaders

CHAPTER 1

Tuesday, September 2, 2008
Las Flores, California

Stella Gonzalez arrived short of breath and ten minutes late for her annual performance review. She sensed it would be her last one. It didn't matter what the human resources department thought of her performance—but she wouldn't divulge that to the perky girl conducting reviews.

The cramped HR trailer at Green Earth Organics was supposed to be temporary but had been there for as long as Stella could remember—fifteen years and counting. It was a ten-minute walk from her workstation on the wash line. Her supervisor had insisted they finish packing the order before he would release her.

Sweating in the ninety-eight-degree heat, she bypassed the line and sat down across the desk from the human resources specialist.

"Sorry I'm late," she said. She took a swig from her water bottle and wiped the sweat off her forehead.

The specialist focused on a piece of paper on her desk and began speaking without looking up.

"You've had a great season, Stella. We want to thank you for all you've done this year to help us make our sales targets. We're giving you a Green Earth Organics travel mug and a copy of *Kate Worthington's Guide to Green Living*. We appreciate your fifteen years of loyal service to the company."

Kate and Roger Worthington were the founders of Green Earth

Organics (called GEO by the local workforce), the nation's largest organic salad company.

She's sticking to the script, Stella thought. *Looks to be about nineteen, maybe twenty years old.*

"Thank you," Stella said.

The girl pushed the paper across the desk and handed Stella a pen.

"Now, if you could just sign on this line, I'll release your gift box, and we'll be all done."

"Is that all?"

"It's a really nice mug. It comes with a detachable spoon so you can use it for soups and things. It's like a Thermos."

"Not the Thermos," Stella said. "It's nice, thank you, but I'm not talking about the mug."

"What is it then? I still have ten more reviews to do before lunch is over."

"It's just ... I thought I heard we might be getting a raise."

"Oh, yes! Sorry, I almost forgot," the specialist said. "Every employee will also get a COLA raise, ten cents per hour. You should see it reflected in next week's check."

Stella nodded. "A COLA."

"That's right. It stands for 'cost of living adjustment.' We want to make sure you can keep up with living expenses."

Stella did the math quickly in her head: ninety cents more a day, less than six dollars a week. It would cover about a gallon and a half of gas.

"I know what COLA stands for. Ten cents more brings me up to eight dollars and fifty cents an hour. I'm really not trying to be difficult here, but I just don't see how you expect us to live on this."

Stella watched the girl fidget in her chair, unprepared to go off script. She probably started less than a year ago and was no doubt making three times as much as the wash liners, or "lifers," as they were known among longtime employees.

"Well, I'll be sure to include your concerns in my monthly report, which management will read. Thank you for your contributions, Stella."

"Gas is four dollars a gallon at the AMPM station in Las Flores, and that's the cheapest in town. That means I have to work five hours just to fill my gas tank."

"As I said, I'll be sure to include your concerns in my monthly report, Stella. Now if you don't mind, I have to move on to my next review. Labor Day put us behind."

Stella stood to leave, wiping her glistening forehead with her scarf.

"Thank you," Stella said. "I would appreciate it if you passed my comments on." She watched the specialist close her folder and add it to the stack on her desk.

Something's got to change, Stella thought as she silently walked by the line of employees snaking out of the trailer. At less than nine dollars an hour, she didn't earn enough to afford California's expensive rents and buy groceries at the same time, not to mention pay for gas for her car. Las Flores was forty-five miles inland from the coast, but it was still close enough to warrant median home prices that topped a half-million dollars. Lifers rented small apartments together or lived in trailer homes converted to farmworker housing.

At five feet two inches and one hundred and forty five pounds, Stella was stout and strong. Fine lines around her eyes and across her forehead were the first signs of aging on an otherwise perfect complexion. At thirty-four, she still looked young but had lived a lot. A light-brown birthmark on her left jawline wrapped behind her ear, and the whites of her eyes stood out against her caramel skin. She looked at others directly when she spoke and was always cordial, even to strangers. Her teeth were white as porcelain, and she never shied away from giving a big smile each time she greeted someone. Stella was popular among her coworkers and always willing to step in if a friend needed help. She was the kind of person who put others first, even at the expense of her own well-being.

Today, she kept her head down and made a beeline back to the lunch trailer. With each step, her thighs rubbed together, creating a rhythmic swish of the lifers' uniform: polyester ski overalls.

Fifteen years. Fifteen years and all they can give me is a cost-of-living adjustment? I thought we were doing so well. They said we made all of our sales targets.

GEO's massive processing facility, known as "the box," was lit with overhead fluorescent tubes that cast a dull glow over the whole space. With the room temperature at twenty degrees, lifers bundled up in layers to keep warm. Employees were human parts, the inner workings of a machine churning out thousands of bagged salads a day.

What am I supposed to do with Kate's book on green living? She should write a book on lean *living, not that she would know the first thing about that.*

Stella and her coworkers smuggled in banned MP3 players, concealed under hairnets covered by headscarves and regulation bump caps. The women used them for entertainment and to avoid hearing male counterparts comment on their bodies. Working to upbeat rhythms of Latina dance music made the hours pass faster and added variety to the assembly line work. Managers occasionally stopped workers to lead hand and arm exercises designed to prevent carpal tunnel syndrome.

Anyone entering the box was required to walk through a sanitation station, gliding hands under sprayers on each side while stepping through a shallow pan of bleach. The concrete floors were slippery and wet with wash water and spilled greens creating a slimy film. Line workers took turns on mop duty, making sure the floor was cleaned to avoid falls. Hanging strips of clear plastic separated one chamber from the next. The smell of chlorine permeated the air. A thirty-minute lunch break at eleven thirty and two other fifteen-minute breaks during the nine-hour shift were mandatory.

Stella carried the gift box under her arm down the long, dim corridor to the lunchroom, passing coworkers returning to the manufacturing floor. Her best friend, Ofelia Bejarano, walked toward her.

"*Hola*, Stella! What did you get?"

"*Navidad en agosto*," she said. "A copy of Kate's book and a coffee mug. Oh, and a COLA raise."

"Ahhh, the annual COLA raise that doesn't even buy a cola!" Ofelia said, laughing.

Ofelia shrugged, put her arm around Stella, and said, "Why do you always expect more, my friend? If you lower your expectations, you wouldn't always be so disappointed."

"My expectations aren't high. I'm tired of working so hard to be poor."

"Well, it's GEO. I don't know why you keep thinking things will change. They never do. And they never will." She pulled Stella closer, put both hands on her shoulders, and looked her friend straight in the eye from an arm's length. "You just have to accept it and move on, guuurl."

The company's mission statement, posted on the walls in the lunchroom and above the wash lines, read: "Our mission is to advance the production of organic agriculture to enrich the earth."

Workers shared their own version, spoken in Spanish among themselves: "Our mission is to advance the production of organic agriculture to enrich the owners."

Stella's job was to cut the butts off romaine lettuce heads for nine hours straight. Tedious as it was, she had decided long ago that sore feet and boredom were small prices to pay if it meant a better future for Esperanza, her only child.

GEO, located in the small, dusty town of Las Flores, was the county's largest private employer. On the outskirts of town, the facility stood like an island fortress in a sea of prime central California farmland. Surrounded by chain-link fences topped with loosely coiled barbed wire, it disrupted tranquil miles of neatly planted lettuce fields and the oak-studded Gabilan and Santa Lucia mountain ranges that wrapped around the fertile farming valley like a maternal hug. At night, the box's lights shone upward, dimming the stars that used to blanket the valley's dark sky.

A guard shack stood at the entrance, staffed by two clipboard-wielding security officers who checked in a constant stream of eighteen-wheelers, employees, and visitors. Strict biosecurity was a recent addition hastily enacted after 9/11. The US Food and Drug Administration had cracked down on manufacturing facilities in the wake of several national outbreaks of foodborne illnesses related to fresh produce.

By the summer of 2008, what was once a hippie, feel-good, back-to-the-land movement was the fastest growing segment of the fresh produce industry—big organic. Increased regulations, the recession, and new competition had cut into GEO's profits over the past ten years. Success came with heightened responsibilities. The company's carefully crafted image could be found on its website and hundreds of news articles covering their meteoric rise to fame during the 1990s. Consumers celebrated the company's social ethic and environmental stewardship.

Old-timers like Stella knew the company's image was a story that resonated with the public but didn't always live up to the promise for employees.

To the dismay of their counterparts in Salinas, California—known as the Salad Bowl of the World—GEO had become the darling of chefs in the San Francisco Bay Area. Iceberg was passé, dethroned by a mixture of delicate baby lettuce leaves, fluffy with opportunity. Spring mix had become the "It Girl" on menus around the country.

GEO capitalized on consumers' growing awareness of their food choices. People wanted to know who grew their food, how it was grown, and how many miles it had traveled to get to their plates. The Food Network propelled a whole new crop of chefs to celebrity status.

Other growers resented GEO for crafting its story at their expense and for marketing the organic designation as superior. "Organic" meant ethical. Fourth-generation growers watched the company's ascent and endured subtle snubs toward farming methods used by their fathers and grandfathers. At coffee shops, growers grumbled that the Worthingtons would still be selling wilted lettuce at farmers' markets had it not been for the ground they had leased them.

It took two newcomers to apply the industrial model to organics. Consumers didn't know that Roger used liquid and powder fertilizers instead of cover crops, or that his fields turned into bare soil wastelands between plantings. Kate made sure that certified organic was associated with fair wages and small farms surrounded by lush hedgerows and fluttering ladybugs.

Lifers cringed at the sight of thousands of aged-out cases discarded daily when some of them went home to empty refrigerators. Stella knew people sitting at the company's desks were paid three times as much as her coworkers who stood all day in a cold box. Still, the job would enable her daughter to live a better life. For her, GEO was the second-to-last leg of a relay race her grandparents had started when they sent their teenage son to the United States to harvest tomatoes in the 1950s. Stella wanted to see Eserpanza cross the finish line, arms raised, smiling and celebrating her family's entrance into the American middle-class. Sweet victory, better than Olympic gold.

After lunch, she returned to her station, consumed with ways to respond to another year without a real raise. Ofelia stood next to her on the wash line.

"Did you know we set a record in sales last quarter?" Stella asked. She whacked the butt off of a romaine bunch and slid the knife across the surface. "And that we're expanding operations to begin producing sliced apples and dried kale? Management says kale is the next big thing, the new spring mix. How could they leave us out again?" *Whack, slide.*

Ofelia slammed the knife down in tandem with Stella. They spoke in Spanish, loud enough to hear each other over the constant hum of processing equipment. When their supervisor, Jimmy Migliozzi, saw them talking he approached with his clipboard and tapped Stella on the shoulder.

"This way, please," he motioned with his index finger. They called him Pinocchio for his big nose and reputation for lying.

Stella looked at Ofelia and rolled her eyes. "Excuse me, Pinocchio is calling me."

Ofelia turned and gave Jimmy a glare, letting him know that she was watching.

"What are you and Ofelia complaining about today?" he asked as he pulled Stella into his office.

Stella stood her ground and replied calmly, thankful he left the door open. Miss September's bronze-oiled and large breasts stood out on the wall calendar hanging behind his desk.

"Nothing, Jimmy."

"You know it's against policy to be discussing reviews, right?" He put his hand on her shoulder and rubbed her upper arm. Stella took a step back.

"We weren't discussing my review," she said.

"Good, because I wouldn't want to have to write you up. You don't have to step away from me like that. I'm not going to hurt you."

"No need to write me up, Jimmy."

He nodded, slowly eyeing her body from head to toe. "Lookin' good, Stella. Hmm. Alright then, get back to work."

She turned to leave as he gave her a light tap on her ass. Stella turned on her heel and slapped his hand away. She walked back to her station where Ofelia was chopping the butts off romaine.

"They hold the carrot out just a centimeter farther, making it impossible to ever take a bite," Ofelia shouted. *Whack, slide.* Stella turned to Ofelia and looked her in the eye.

"I'm going to start my own farming business, one where I can set my own hours—or at least go by Mother Nature's hours—and choose my clients."

"Doing what?" Ofelia asked. "You have bills to pay, girl!"

"I'm going to plant edible gardens for people too busy to do it themselves but who want fresh vegetables. Then they won't need to buy these bagged salads."

Ofelia smirked and rolled her eyes. "Kind of like *gardening*?"

"No. It's more than a garden," Ofelia said. "It's farming, home farming."

"You do that," Ofelia said, laughing. "But you better grow some food for yourself for when you have no money to buy any!"

"I'm going to do it, you'll see," Stella said. "I've already helped some people plant tomatoes and peppers during the off-season and they paid me well."

The wash line employees were trained to be efficient, chopping at the precise spot where the core softens and the leaves begin. In two swoops, workers drop the blade and sweep the butts into thirty-two-gallon plastic garbage bins. Outer leaves are removed and then the hearts are placed on a conveyer belt to be packed, shipped, and sold for five dollars and fifty cents a bag in stores nationwide. Such efficiencies made the idea of putting organic lettuce into a plastic bag a billion-dollar industry. Stella could never decide if they were selling lettuce or convenience. It was the chopping, washing, and bagging that made the leaves so expensive.

"People pay more for GEO's washed salads, why wouldn't they pay someone to grow it right in their own yard?" Stella asked. "It would be even fresher."

"I know you never planned to be at GEO for this long," Ofelia said. "But this job is familiar and steady. GEO has hired us back year after year. Whether you like or not, we are tied to this place. This job enables you to pay your rent and save something toward Esperanza's education."

"We put in as many hours as the office girls. They can afford to send their children to college, but we can't even fill our gas tanks. Why should their children's futures be brighter than ours?"

Stella slid romaine butts into awaiting bins for another three hours. *Whack. Slide. Whack. Slide.* Her knife hit the cutting surface hard. Each chop felt good. She hummed to the music in her headphones.

"You're on fire today," Ofelia said. "Are you pretending that is Pinocchio's head?" They laughed out loud together.

It will be different for Esperanza. I may not have had a lot of choices, but my daughter will.

After their shift, they changed out of their white smocks and collected their lunch boxes from the cubby wall.

"We made all of our targets. What does it take to get ahead?" Stella said.

"I never thought I'd say this, but maybe it's time to start listening to Emiliano," Ofelia said. "There! I said it, just don't tell anyone I told you to do something so stupid."

Stella nodded with a knowing smile. "I'm even more surprised to hear you say that than you are, but I think you might be right."

CHAPTER 2

Jane Janhusen awoke to her cell phone vibrating on the nightstand next to her bed. She fumbled for it in the morning dimness, pressed the on button, and read the illuminated screen's latest e-mail thread through a dissipating fog of sleep. Kate's response was on top.

> From: Kate Worthington
> Sent: Tuesday, September 2, 2008, 6:29 a.m.
> To: Caroline Boyd; Jane Janhusen
> Subject: Re: Conference call tomorrow
>
> You are supposed to indulge my request and e-mail it to me so I don't need to dig up old e-mails. Haven't you figured that out yet?
>
> -----Original Message-----
> From: Caroline Boyd
> Sent: Tuesday, September 2, 2008, 6:28 a.m.
> To: Kate Worthington; Jane Janhusen
> Subject: Re: Conference call tomorrow
>
> Yes, Kate, it's on the agenda.
> Caroline Boyd, Green Earth Organics
> Sent from my Verizon Wireless BlackBerry
>
> ----- Original Message -----
> From: Kate Worthington
> To: Jane Janhusen; Caroline Boyd

Sent: Monday, September 1, 2008, 10:08 p.m.
Subject: Conference call tomorrow

Hi,
I will be able to call in from 12:00–12:30. Is there a # I
should use? Are there other call-ins?
Thanks,
Kate

Jane shook her head and sighed.

Such a rookie move, Caroline.

That counted as a mortal sin in Kate's world.

After ten years, Jane had secured a place in Roger and Kate's inner circle. She had watched Kate struggle to hold on to her early fame and now saw her clinging to a diminished role in the booming organic industry. Jane's focus was to help Kate transition from organic pioneer to up-and-coming celebrity foodie matron. With so many others in the space, Kate's influence was fading. Jane's job was to stop the inevitable.

"I'm gonna get an earful about *that*," she said to her cat.

The cat purred and rubbed against Jane's leg.

"I wish everyone were as content as you."

She lifted the cat and stroked her behind the ears before doing a few simple yoga stretches.

In the shower, she pondered her position. GEO was flying high. Sales were at record levels and growing 20 percent "year over year" as Roger liked to say. They were just shy of hitting the $500-million milestone in annual sales, the sweet spot that would begin attracting private equity firms and enable Roger to activate his long-awaited exit strategy. Jane called the firms "vulture capitalists" and accused them of circling above companies with potential, waiting to swoop in and replace management with their own people. Roger loved the idea of wooing Wall Street and dreamed of working with his idols in the private equity world, just a few miles north on Sand Hill Road.

Sales were expected to pick up after the summer lull, when farmers' markets collapsed their E-Z UP canopies and shut down for the season. "Local" was becoming more and more of a problem for GEO as consumers began to calculate the carbon footprint of shipping washed greens in plastic from the Salinas Valley to Manhattan. It grated on Jane's nerves when she heard colleagues debating the pros and cons of local versus organic. She hated the term "food miles." The controversy crept up more often these days as foodie activist movies and the Food Network gained cult followings. Disassociating GEO's industrial organic model from the public's growing distaste for plastic packaging was her latest obsession.

She dried off and walked over to her closet to choose the day's outfit. Jane was petite but strong. She wore her shoulder-length, brunette hair pulled back in a tight, low ponytail. Because she was barely five feet and a female manager in the male-dominated produce industry, she always dressed professionally, affecting an air of authority despite buried insecurities. Her wardrobe consisted of a collection of size six Theory skirts and blazers, J.Crew gray pants, black pumps with minimum three-inch heels, and white Lycra tank tops, which she ordered in bulk from the Ann Taylor website bookmarked on her laptop. She rotated a variety of cardigan sweaters paired with fake pearls. Unlike Kate, Jane wore makeup to accentuate her features and never forgot to put on her imitation Cartier tank watch.

The only time Jane did not assert her authority was around Kate, and that was deliberate. Although she spoke up in front of her boss, she knew better than to overshadow her. When she interviewed for the copy editor job back in 1998, GEO's annual sales were still under $100 million. The company's relatively small size gave her close access to Kate, whom she had idolized from afar as an organic pioneer and female role model. For her initial interview with the company, Jane was surprised to meet with Kate—the *founder* of Green Earth Organics! At forty, Jane was nine years younger than Kate, but she felt almost like a daughter, watching and learning from day one.

She chose a simple white tank top and navy pencil skirt. Her first task of the day would be to assure Kate that Caroline was not purposely dodging a request. Then she would tell Caroline that replying to e-mails from Kate without an answer was unacceptable.

CHAPTER 3

Santa Lucinda, California

Kate Worthington had it all, or at least it looked that way. At forty-nine, she was attractive, self-assured, and successful. Her slight frame, freckles, and curly auburn hair gave her a natural look. At the advice of her naturopath, she favored henna over chemical hair color. Her looks remained youthful while Roger had developed a bulge over his belt and side part that kept creeping closer to his ears. Sales reps took bets on whether or not he colored the dirty blonde combover.

She had worked hard to get where she was. She and Roger spent years building Green Earth Organics. Their employee base had grown to almost 2,000, and she had established herself as a true organic pioneer. In magazine articles and radio and television interviews, she was the picture of a confident, mission-driven business owner. Privately though she obsessed over ensuring her status as the Mother of the Organic Movement. Every week, she reviewed clipped articles about organics compiled by her team and neatly placed in plastic sleeves of her media binder. As the organic segment grew, so did her competition. Others were crowding her stage, and she could feel her early notoriety slipping away. It had been almost twenty years since she and Roger started the company, and imitators had popped up everywhere. Even the big, conventional salad companies were starting organic lines driving the price down and, in her mind, polluting the purity of the label.

GEO's marketing department was entirely Kate's domain. She set all the policies and spent her days surrounded by a tight orbit of carefully chosen, trusted advisors. Fifty miles west of the Las Flores manufacturing plant, the marketing office was in the historic mission town of Santa Lucinda along California's famous scenic coastline. Santa Lucinda was perched at the edge of the continent overlooking the Pacific's distant horizon. Water stretched as far west as the eye could see. The possibilities were endless from that point of view.

Kate loved the space. It was the antithesis of the dusty, noisy processing plant in Las Flores. "Marketing," for short, was library quiet, modern, and clean with a minimalistic interior bathed in natural light. When they moved in, Jane had asked the facilities department crew to hang bright Matisse and Delaunay prints on the walls, all painted in natural tones of eggshell green and butter yellow. Sisal runners, emitting a calming, earthy fennel aroma, softened the bamboo flooring in the hallways. Oversize glass vases of seasonal foliage, delivered weekly from GEO's nearby retail store, the Roadside Stand, were placed on tables throughout the building, adding more fragrant overtones. Floor-to-ceiling windows lined the conference room and Kate's office, which looked out on a statuesque cluster of valley oaks. More than anything, the trees were why she had chosen the building.

Glass desktops free of clutter dotted a shared, open workspace. Most desks sported only sleek new MacBook Pros, Apple's latest must-have toy. Kate liked her environment sparse and quiet with the exception of an occasional relaxation CD murmuring softly from an invisible Bose sound system. Staffers knew to keep their voices down and chatter to a minimum, even around the water cooler.

Staff meetings took place daily at 10:00 a.m. sharp. Jane was always there twenty minutes early. The two met before the staff convened so Jane could update Kate on issues and feed her any gossip floating around the office or at the plant in Las Flores.

Trustworthy Jane. She had worked directly with Kate and Roger for ten years, successfully building a strategic wall of defense around them, deftly intercepting all incoming missiles from competitors, unions, government regulators, and increasingly annoying reporters with an agenda.

Who would have thought one day I wouldn't want to talk to a reporter? Or consider an environmentalist an annoyance?

How times were changing. It seemed the more successful GEO became, the more attacks they had to fend off.

Kate always turned to Jane for comfort and reassurance that all was good in GEO's universe. Jane's corporate look was a stark contrast to Kate, who favored a more relaxed, Mother Earth style. They complemented each other well, with Jane acting as GEO's corporate female spokesperson and Kate personifying the antiestablishment organic label. They were an effective tag team that served the company's diverse interests well. GEO was represented by one or the other, depending on the event. She rearranged the photos and paperweight on her desk, annoyed with the cleaning crew for moving them each night. Jane breezed in right on time.

"Do you think they leave everything slightly askew just to let me know they were here? I mean, really, *why* do they always have to move *everything* on my desk?"

"I'll talk to facilities about that," Jane said.

"We need to purchase eight hundred more copies of my book to give to our sales employees for the holidays."

"Yep. I've got Caroline on it."

"*Care*-o-line!" Kate spat. "Did you see her reply to my e-mail this morning?"

"Yes, I did. She was just trying to be responsive, Kate. She probably didn't have the number handy. I'll talk to her about it. She's a smart cookie. She'll learn from her mistakes."

Jane shook her head mildly and gave Kate her signature "If-I-don't-do-it, no-one-else-will" look. Kate relaxed a notch and even flashed a hint of a smile. Jane the Fixer.

Jane had made herself indispensable to the Worthingtons. With one sigh, she could plant a seed in Kate's head that others weren't holding their weight and could not be trusted.

"The books are a tax write-off, right? And a nice gift for all of our employees," Kate said.

"Yep."

"Good. My publisher will be thrilled with the bump in sales."

Kate smiled, this time more broadly, pleased for having accomplished three tasks at once: tax write-off, employee holiday gifts, and accolades from her publisher for getting closer to their sales targets. She turned toward Jane with an expectant look.

"What's next?"

Jane picked up the hardbound *Kate Worthington's Guide to Green Living* from her desk. Kate had worked on it for more than a year, consulting everyone from graphic designers to climate scientists to get everything just right.

"Employees are loving it. We're distributing copies to line workers this week as we conduct performance reviews. It's been a good way to connect to our hourly employees. You might want to think about penciling in some time to go out to the plant and do a book signing. I know your schedule is tight, but it really boosts morale. They love to see you in person. Remember, they are your biggest fans, after our customers." She set the book back down on Kate's desk.

"I'll think about it. I've heard murmurs about union activity. Do you think employees are thinking of organizing? Why would they want to do that? We've been so good to them."

"I haven't heard much about that in recent months, but I'll ask around. These rumors come and go in cycles every couple of years. I wouldn't worry about it."

Kate crossed her arms and began nibbling on her left pinkie fingernail—a defensive tic Jane noticed whenever Kate was nervous. Her smile vanished.

"I know you dread the idea of making small talk with so many employees and having to shake all their hands," Jane said. "But you know how important it is to have face time with the line workers."

"In my next book, I want to tell my side of the organic story and not allow those environmental or consumer groups to frame the discussion.

We need to *own* the message. GEO will *not* be in the position of defending the use of plastic packaging. We need to talk about how we are using *sustainable* plastic. You know, put a positive spin on it. It's the only way to expand our reach. I want people to praise us for using recycled plastic instead of criticizing us for filling landfills."

"Right," Jane said.

"Sustainable plastic. Industrial organic. Those pesky oxymorons. We need to get ahead of them."

"Exactly."

"How is the employee meeting coming along? Are we still on for October?"

"Yes, October works well. I'm thinking of using the meeting as a platform to educate our workforce about our commitment to the environment."

"Do you know anyone at *Fast Company*? I saw Nell Newman on the cover at the supermarket the other day. Why should Newman's Own Organics get the cover and not us? We're much bigger."

Jane tried to keep up with Kate's stream of consciousness, a habit when Kate was nervous, which seemed to be all the time lately.

"I don't have a contact at *Fast Company*. But I can look into it. I might know someone who can introduce me."

The fog outside was beginning to thin as patches of blue sky peeked through its veil. The oaks began to take on more color and depth. It was early in the day for the fog to be lifting. Only 9:45 a.m. and already 65 degrees.

"How is this heat affecting quality?" Kate asked

"We're harvesting before dawn and packing like crazy. Orders are strong," Jane said. "Every wash line is running at full capacity, per Roger's direction."

"Good. Let's move those salads out the door. On our way to five hundred million."

CHAPTER 4

Tipton, Iowa

The Tuesday after Labor Day was like every other day in the Malmquist household. Their small kitchen was filled with toddlers competing for their parents' attention. Crayon drawings were taped to the walls and squished milk-soaked Cheerios splattered across the linoleum floor. Ruth Malmquist was diligent about nutrition. She blended bananas, apple juice, yogurt, and raw spinach into smoothies for her ruddy-faced crew. They sucked down "Mommy's Superman shakes," tipping their sippy cups in the air as they kicked against their high chairs.

She had married her high school sweetheart, Scott Malmquist, shortly after graduation. He was the star quarterback and she the head cheerleader, known as Barbie and Ken. She was nineteen when the first baby arrived. They had settled down in a small house on the outskirts of Cedar Rapids, Iowa, surrounded by their families.

By the time her youngest was born, the Malmquists were parents to four children under the age of six: Bucky, five, Brady, three, Brian, two, and finally a daughter, Brianna, eleven months. Ruth was twenty-five.

"Yum! Finish your Mommy's Superman shakes, and you'll be strong like Daddy!" Ruth said.

She removed the grimy high chair tray and hoisted Brianna up by the armpits, raising her into the air to give her a loud smooch on her fat, sticky baby cheek.

"Whose my tasty baby? Mmmmmmm. Tasty baby!"

Brianna giggled and squirmed out of her mother's arms, her big blue eyes following her older brothers.

"Boys, keep an eye on your sister!"

Brianna scooted across the floor on all fours like a monkey. She knew how to walk, but it was much faster to crawl, and she was eager to catch up with her brothers who were heading outside to play.

Ruth detached the blender from its base and rinsed the plastic pitcher in hot, sudsy water before placing it on the drying rack. She always cleaned up the kitchen before putting the baby down for her morning nap, knowing that lunch would be easier to prepare if she started with a clean counter. She rolled the top of the spinach bag, fastened it with a plastic clip, and placed it back in the refrigerator. She used the remaining leaves for a dinner salad each night.

As she stood at the sink looking out the window, Ruth watched Scott and the kids chase one another around their small lawn—a daily ritual in the summer—and smiled with contentment. Life had given her everything she had dreamed of. They lived simply on Scott's $30,000 annual salary. When the local school district told them Bucky would be bused across town for kindergarten, they decided to homeschool. The choice allowed them more time together as a family and let Ruth weave their Mormon faith into his curriculum.

Scott barreled through the screen door, baby in arms and dragging a laughing boy on each ankle. His athletic frame still made her heart flutter. He kissed her on the cheek and handed off the baby like a football before grabbing his keys.

"Gotta run, honey. Be home in a few. Boys! Be good for your mother!"

Scott always came home for lunch, a perk of his job as a grocery clerk at the local Hy-Vee grocery store in nearby Cedar Rapids.

"Bye, sweetie. Love ya bunches," Ruth said.

She turned her face to meet him for a kiss. Scott pecked her on the cheek and grabbed his wallet and car keys before leaving.

"Back atcha, babe."

He always winked at her when he said that. Ruth admired his biceps, stretching the sleeve of his T-shirt, as he skipped out the door. Scanning the half-cleaned-up kitchen, she decided it was more important to keep to Brianna's nap schedule than scrub down the floor and counters.

"I'm going to put the baby down for a nap, boys. Play nicely outside for a few minutes, and then I'll be down to read before quiet time, okay?"

"Okay, Mama!" Bucky yelled. "I'm in charge!"

Ruth's routine was solid. She had mastered the schedules of four children, always conscious that it was important to have individual time with each one. The baby still took two naps a day, and Brian, the two-year-old, was down to one long afternoon nap. While he napped, the older boys spent an hour of quiet time coloring or having Ruth read to them. She learned from her mother and mother-in-law, each the mother of six, that having a regular routine was the only way to survive.

They talked about having more children, but decided to wait until Brianna was two before trying again. Scott's job didn't seem to be at risk. Still, they had watched as friends had lost jobs that seemed secure. They had purchased their house for $100,000 with 30 percent down and were keeping up on mortgage payments, but the adjustable loan they took out in 2005 was set to increase as interest rates went up. They didn't believe in living beyond their means and wanted to make sure they didn't get in over their heads. Always cautious. Scott was fond of espousing simple rules to live by. His mantra, repeated every time they were tempted to overspend, was "No cashy, no splashy! Except for houses and cars. That's good debt, as long as it's a used Honda, pre-owned certified of course." Ruth loved his pragmatic approach to life.

She finished nursing the baby and put her down for a nap in her bassinet at the foot of their bed. She went back downstairs to check on the boys, who were unusually quiet.

"What's wrong with you?" she said. Bucky lay curled on the floor, clutching his arms over his stomach.

"My tummy hurts, Mama."

CHAPTER 5

Santa Lucinda Golf and Country Club was one of Roger's favorite places. Clusters of brown distressed leather chairs and oversize ottomans surrounded an imposing stone fireplace at one end of the lobby, giving it an old boys' club feel. Solid old-growth redwood beams stretched overhead. Gold-framed paintings of famous golf courses lined the wood-paneled walls, and oriental carpets covered the wide-plank oak floors. The room smelled of expensive colognes. Fresh-cut oversize floral arrangements adorned a large center table and side tables along the walls.

It was here where Roger let loose and bounced ideas off his golf buddies, a foursome comprised of two attorney friends and his younger brother, Tony, a manager in GEO's sales department. Their weekly round granted Roger a welcomed respite from the office and a safe venue for discussions of everything from pending business deals to marriage counseling. No subject was off limits.

The weather was record-setting hot, but that didn't stop the foursome from teeing off at 11:00 a.m. sharp for their weekly round. They emerged from the clubhouse, squinting in the light gleaming off the Pacific Ocean below, and walked to the first hole.

Roger's driver made an audible whoosh before striking the ball at its sweet spot with a piercing ping. It soared long and straight, then bounced a couple of times before rolling to a graceful stop a few feet from the green.

"Why can't I hit it like that every time?" Roger said.

"It's all that tension at work. You're taking it out on the ball," Tony said.

"We got a noise complaint at Las Flores last week. I'm just waiting for the first workers' comp claim to roll in on *that* one. They'd win some settlement cash from us, don't you think?"

"Hmmm, depends on their attorney," Michael said. "You're right, they probably have a case. You should fix the noise levels before someone does sue you, or at least provide them with ear plugs."

Michael Hardy, an old friend of Roger's from GEO's early days, was an estate attorney in Santa Lucinda, catering to rich widows and young entrepreneurs. His partner, Peter Duffy, represented some of Roger's competitors in the Salinas Valley on real estate deals and farming leases. Their firm, Hardy & Duffy, was known for turning farmers into developers. Michael was fond of noting that every smart farmer's last crop was houses.

Maybe I should go into corporate litigation. I could rack up hundreds of billable hours defending you," Michael said.

Peter rolled his eyes.

"Nah. Hardy & Duffy is too small for Kate and Roger. They like working with all those fancy San Francisco firms." He shook his head and lined up his driver.

"I think divorce law would be more profitable," Roger said. He wiped a bead of sweat from the tip of his nose.

Michael turned to face Roger. "Really? Is Kate planning to leave you? You realize she would have the stronger case."

"Let's just say that GEO's public relations strategy is preserving my marriage."

"But is the PR strategy helping your *sex life*?" Tony asked.

"Not the one with my wife," Roger said.

"You gotta stop eating all that organic shit, dude. It's making you soft. GMOs are better than Viagra," Tony said.

Peter laughed and flexed a bicep, nodding in agreement. "I can attest to that."

"Fuck you. *I'm* not the one who needs sexual coaching. And why do you always have to be so vulgar?" Roger said.

"Maybe the little woman's unimpressed with your ol' salad-fed cock. A little growth hormone in your steak might be just what the doc ordered. I'm telling you: it works for me every time," Tony said.

"Yeah, apparently my whole sales department knows about that too. Can we talk about something else?" Roger said. "You guys aren't exactly marital role models." He looked directly at his twice-divorced brother.

"I'm just sayin'. You're the one who brought it up," Tony said. Michael teed off, and the foursome loaded their golf bags into the cart.

"I hear Bear Stearns is just the first of the major investment banks to go belly-up," Peter said.

"JP Morgan stole it," Michael said.

"Waiting for the next shoe to drop," Peter said.

"Nah, the Feds will always step in," Michael said. "They ponied up twenty-nine billion to save Bear Stearns. They're not going to let these other guys fail. Too many American jobs at stake."

"How do you think it's going to affect IPOs? Or M and A activity?"

"Too soon to tell," Michael said. "I imagine a lot of deals will be put on hold as investors sit tight. They get jittery pretty easily."

They each took turns putting.

"Stocks are risky. I'll stick with food. People are always going to buy good food. Our current plan is to take GEO beyond produce," Roger said. "We've built the nation's largest organic food company, with new product lines rolling out monthly. I want to cash in before the market changes."

"That's what Bear Stearns wanted too," Peter said. "Their stock price went from one hundred and fifty-nine dollars to two dollars in one year. You better get moving."

"They got ten dollars in the end," Michael said.

"Those guys knew they were selling junk. I actually have a good product to sell—healthy food—and a brand people trust. Thanks to Kate."

"Yeah, well, I wouldn't count on anything until you have a check in your hand," Peter said. He tapped the ball before it rolled toward the hole and spun around the cup without going in. "Damn it. I can't find the hole today."

"Put a little hair around it," Tony said. "It's always easy to find then." The four of them erupted in laughter.

"What are you? Sixteen?" Peter said.

"I got you to laugh, didn't I?"

"Have you guys heard enough of Tony's juvenile male humor yet?" Roger asked. "I have to get back to the office."

CHAPTER 6

Tipton, Iowa

"Let me rub your belly," Ruth said.

She knelt down and put her hand on Bucky's stomach.

"It hurts, Mama." He moaned, rolling from side to side.

"It's a little tummy ache. Let's have some quiet time, and I'll read you a book. Which one do you want to read?"

"Lowly!" Brady offered. "He likes Lowly!"

"Good pick. I love that one."

Ruth loved Richard Scarry books. The detailed illustrations mesmerized the children who delighted in looking for Lowly Worm on every page.

Bucky scrambled up onto the sofa and curled into his mother's lap like a sleeping puppy as she began to read *Busiest Firefighters Ever*. But his stomach wasn't calming down. He writhed in pain, contorted and groaning.

"Mama, I have to poop."

She carried Bucky to the bathroom. Fumbling in a messy bathroom drawer, she pulled out a thermometer and held it in his mouth while he sat on the toilet, moaning in pain. One hundred and two degrees. When she saw blood in his diarrhea, she went to the kitchen to find the doctor's number, written neatly on an index card with other emergency numbers and taped inside a cabinet. The phone rang several times.

"Dr. Joseph Ryan's office. Please hold." *Click.* Ruth heard the phone switch to Muzak before she could respond. When the woman came back on the line, she sounded rushed.

"Thank you for holding."

"Hi, this is Ruth Malmquist. My son is complaining of stomach pain, and it doesn't seem to be—"

"Does he have a fever? Diarrhea?"

"Yes and yes. And a fever of a hundred and two."

"Okay, please hold while I check the schedule."

Ruth waited again. Bucky was lying on the couch, lethargic and pale. She held the phone, breathing calmly and rubbing his back while he moaned.

"The doctor says to give him some Imodium for the diarrhea and clear liquids to keep him hydrated through the night. Call us in the morning if there's no improvement," the receptionist said.

"I'm doing all that," Ruth said. "I'll call back in an hour if he's not better." She hung up, annoyed.

"It hurts, Mama."

He was contorted and clutching his abdomen as Ruth soothed him.

Brady watched from the family room floor, mesmerized by Sponge Bob on the television

"What's wrong with Bucky, Mama?" Brady asked. "He looks sick."

"He's got a little tummy ache, sweetie, but he'll be okay. Don't worry."

Ruth waited forty-five minutes before calling the doctor back.

"I'd rather not wait until tomorrow. I think the doctor should see him today," she told the receptionist. "He's not getting any better, and I don't want to end up in the emergency room in the middle of the night."

A nurse practitioner asked her more questions about what Bucky had eaten and told her to put him on a BRAT diet until his symptoms improved.

"He usually loves all those things, but he has no appetite," Ruth said. "He won't even look at a banana."

The nurse put her on hold again. Ruth waited, rubbing Bucky's back until the nurse came back on.

"Okay, Dr. Ryan would like you to bring him in."

She hung up the phone and grabbed a Raffi CD, the boys' favorite, to play in the minivan. After dressing the baby, she loaded the children into their car seats and tried to distract Bucky, who was still holding his stomach and moaning.

"Let's listen to 'Wheels on the Bus'!" Ruth said.

She pulled the minivan out of their driveway and headed north on Highway 38 for the forty-five-minute drive to Cedar Rapids.

Bucky usually smiled and sang along, but Ruth watched him in her rearview mirror. His eyes were weary, and his body was limp with exhaustion. He looked like a rag doll. When they arrived at St. Luke's Hospital in Cedar Rapids she unloaded the baby first, strapping her face toward her chest into a BabyBjörn carrier. Bucky was barely awake and still moaning. The other boys scrambled out of the van and marched into the hospital behind their mother like well-behaved ducklings.

When they were called in, Dr. Ryan asked her the standard questions, reading his scribbled notes aloud to Ruth.

"09/02/08, 2:00 p.m. Appears lethargic upon arrival. Fever 101.8°F."

"He's been complaining of a bad stomachache, and his diarrhea hasn't stopped all day," Ruth said. "At one point, I just laid on the bathroom floor with him to be near the toilet."

"I'm going to advise some lab tests. I'd like to take a blood sample and take a stool specimen for testing. We'll need to admit him and start IV fluids in order to prevent dehydration. Don't worry, Mom, he's in good hands here." Dr. Ryan snapped his folder shut and gave her a reassuring pat on the shoulder.

"Should I call my husband to have him meet me here and take the other children home?

"That would be a good idea. This may take a while."

CHAPTER 7

After her meeting with Jane, Kate sat in her office looking out at the oak trees and listening to the waves crash on the beach two blocks away. Despite her laid-back appearance, Kate was wound tight. She controlled the marketing department with the precision of a laser beam. Her constant revisions to everything from the romantic copy on the company's organic raisins packaging to their Facebook page responses meant that staff could not be too tied to their own ideas.

She turned on the screen to her Apple desktop. Her phone buzzed.

"Kate, it's Jane. I forgot to ask if you've reviewed Roger's talking points for his interview with *Forbes* next week? I want to make sure you and Roger are on the same page and comfortable with all the facts before we get on the phone with the reporter. I've looked into some of his previous articles. He's going to ask about how increased fuel costs are cutting into our profits and if we think our reliance on plastic packaging is a sustainable business model. The price of oil hit one hundred and fifty dollars a barrel yesterday. Blah, blah, blah. I get so tired of journalists thinking they're ahead of the rest of us all the time."

"What's his angle?"

Kate logged on and went straight to GEO's Roadside Stand Facebook page. There were twenty-five notifications in the upper right corner. Jane was still talking.

"Food miles is becoming an issue. I'm hearing more buzz about the distance between where things are grown and where they're purchased. Do they not get that you can't buy spring mix in Michigan or New York in the winter? We can only grow this stuff year-round in California and Arizona. I also found a book he wrote a few years ago on how plastic bottles are polluting the nation's waterways and killing marine life. He wrote an article in *The Atlantic* on how green companies like Method and Patagonia are using plastic from those garbage islands in the Pacific to package their cleaning products and make fleece jackets."

"Really? They're sending boats all the way out in the ocean to source plastic for their ugly clothes? I'm reading our Facebook page right now, and someone posted a picture of one of our clamshells with a comment that says, *'Mother Nature's balsamic vinegar cleans these greens better than chlorine and plastic packaging.'*"

"What's her point?"

"Vinegar kills bacteria. Are we still using chlorine?"

"Until we find something better. Vinegar doesn't kill E.coli."

Clamshells were GEO's favored packaging option. The clear shoe-box-shaped package kept the leaves fluffy and dry, but environmentalists hated them.

"He didn't mention clamshells, but we should be prepared for that."

Kate studied the picture of one of GEO's clamshells. It was lying on top of a pile of garbage. Another shot showed GEO's raisins and sliced apples all packed in plastic.

"Hmmm. That is a lot of plastic. A lot of people are liking it. I wonder if this could grow legs. I love social media until it turns on you. You can re-use our clamshells as shoeboxes, are we telling people that? Let's post a picture of a closet filled with our clamshells as shoeboxes."

The marketing department consisted of six women. They monitored GEO's Twitter and Facebook feeds, submitted the Worthingtons' names to high-profile award contests, and collected press clippings.

"Our messaging to the *Forbes* reporter is this: *'We're participating in a larger production cycle, making the whole system more efficient,'*" Jane said.

"We're so ahead of everyone else in the industry. We've always been pioneers. Thought leaders. Innovators."

"Yep. I'll fine-tune the talking points to incorporate those themes.

Oh, and on the union rumors—you're right. A group has been meeting secretly during breaks and after shifts in the parking lot."

"Well, that needs to stop," Kate said. "What are we doing about it?"

"I'm talking over options with HR. We're thinking of putting together a PowerPoint educating employees on what unions are."

"And what they aren't," Kate said. "They'll only take money out of paychecks and not give anything in return. We are good to our employees. Why would they want to unionize?"

"It's probably just noise from a few activist types," Jane said. "Don't worry. We're on it."

Marketing stayed away from the manufacturing side of the business. Kate saw the brand as an extension of herself, something she had given birth to and raised to maturity, as sacred as a firstborn. Her interest, and therefore involvement, in operations was less passionate. She was happy to turn that part of the business over to Roger.

"One more thing. Your nomination for National Organic Partnership's Woman of the Year. I'm almost ready to submit. I've answered all the questions about your history and why you and Roger decided to go organic, but I'm not sure what to say about where you see the industry going in the next five to ten years. Any thoughts on that?"

"Organics will only keep growing as people realize the harmful side effects of pesticides on our bodies and the soil. I see organics growing every year, and more companies starting their own organic lines, following Roger's and my lead. How ya like dem apples?"

Jane laughed politely.

"Dem apples are good. Last thing, the employee meeting. Do we want to go with a theme this year? I'm confirming October, before the move."

GEO made a biannual sojourn to Yuma, Arizona, known simply as "the move," when they transported hundreds of truckloads of machinery and set up manufacturing operations closer to irrigated lettuce fields in the Arizona desert.

"Why don't we showcase our sustainable packaging at that meeting?" Kate said.

"I like it," Jane said. "May even attract some good press. What about having a wash-line worker speak about quality control on the Las Flores plant floor?"

"Yes, I like the idea of celebrating every step of our processes from field to processing to packing. Let's try to find a lifer, someone who has been with us from the start. I'll think about a book signing too. If we do that, be sure to have hand sanitizer. You know the one I like, with the moisturizing organic lavender oil in it."

"Yes, of course."

The employee meeting had evolved over the years into a gala showcase with Kate and Roger speaking before twelve hundred employees. Roger used it as his IPO prep, sauntering back and forth across the stage, his image projected on a huge screen behind him like he'd seen Steve Jobs and Larry Ellison do at their annual shareholder meetings. Kate teased him for wearing a black mock turtleneck.

They cleared out part of the manufacturing plant and set up a stage in front of long tables for lunch. Separated by forty-five miles, marketing and operations were two different worlds that worked better when kept apart. Jane split her time between two offices, one in Santa Lucinda and one in Las Flores.

"Okay, I think we're done. I'll ask HR to find a line worker to speak and have Caroline look into renting tables and get started on the menu. Do you have anything else?"

"No, I just want to be sure Roger is ready for the *Forbes* interview. That's going to be important. You know he's preparing a road show with potential buyers, right?"

"I'm meeting with him this afternoon to go over the talking points. No worries, Kate."

"Good. Being featured in *Forbes* will be a key milestone for GEO. A cover story would be nice. See if you can get them to use *visionary* before Roger's name."

"I'll see what I can do."

"Remember I'm not going to be able to make the marketing meeting this morning. I have a call with the bankers."

"No problem. I'll let everyone know. I'm headed over to Las Flores this afternoon. We're trying to work more closely with sales. I'll have my cell if you need me."

CHAPTER 8

Curved like a horseshoe so traffic flowed during pickup and drop-off, the driveway in front of Las Flores High School encircled a feeble patch of dried-up lawn. Stella joined the line of cars that snaked around it and waited for her daughter to emerge. She watched the stay-at-home moms, with their designer handbags and oversize sunglasses, park their Suburbans and gather around a bench under an imposing oak tree. They laughed and gossiped.

What do they do all day? Stella thought. *Must be nice to have every day free, with time to clean the house, plan and cook dinner, or read a book. They probably don't even cook or clean their own homes. Maybe they work out or shop with the money their husbands give them. Imagine, just having money appear in your bank account every month.*

The line moved forward, and a loud honk behind her jolted her out of her daydream.

Stop staring, Stella.

Her 1988 Honda Prelude was not the most expensive in the line, but she kept it immaculate, and it was reliable. Its faded red paint was chipped. She changed the oil religiously and carried quarters with her to use at the gas station vacuum on the worn beige cloth seats and floor mats.

Stella beamed as she watched Esperanza skip toward the car. Esperanza was a star setter on the high school volleyball team and a straight-A student. At seventeen, she was the same age as Stella was when she gave birth to her. Stella was doing everything she could to avoid a repeated surprise with her daughter.

"Hola, *mija*."

Esperanza opened the back door to throw her backpack on the seat before climbing into the passenger seat. Stella liked to use some Spanish, hoping to feed the language neurons in her daughter's brain.

"Cómo estuvo el día?" Stella asked.

"Okay," Esperanza said.

She flashed a wide smile inherited from her mother.

"I got an A on my Algebra quiz!"

"Bien por ti! Sabía que podías hacerlo."

"Now I just have to get through next week's history quiz, and then I'm going to focus on volleyball tryouts."

"You will do it, *mija*. I have been praying about it, and I can feel your success."

"Thanks, Mama, but I don't need your prayers. I work hard!"

"Prayers don't hurt."

"What's this?"

Esperanza leaned down to lift the flaps on the cardboard gift box.

"Oh, it's my annual gift from GEO. They want us to know how much we're appreciated."

Esperanza examined Kate's book. *"Kate Worthington's Guide to Green Living.* Does her private plane run on biodiesel or something?" she asked.

"Ah, *mija*. Always so observant! How do you know she has a private plane?"

"I don't. But I bet she does!"

She put the box in the backseat and pulled the seat belt across her chest, clicking it into place while she waved good-bye to her friends on the curb.

"I am going to make honor roll again, Mama. Let's go to The Centre."

The Centre was a misnomer, not only because of its pretentious French spelling, but its location on the outskirts of Las Flores.

Esperanza's father had run off with another woman before she was born. Still, Stella refused to allow single parenthood to dampen her excitement at becoming a mother, even if she was just seventeen. She managed without him and was even thankful at times that her paychecks weren't going to buy beer she didn't drink and cigarettes she didn't smoke. After Esperanza was born, Stella adopted a simple routine: work, eat, sleep, repeat. They lived with her mother. The three women fit together like a garlic bulb, nestled in the same skin but also beautiful as separate cloves. *Gran* was Esperanza's first word. They lived in a tiny, rented house on the outskirts of Las Flores. Gran cooked and she was good at it. On weeknights, she wrapped homemade tortillas around slow-cooked pork, rice, and beans to pack burritos for her girls' lunches. She taught Esperanza how to make them too:

Whisk the flour, salt, and baking powder together in a mixing bowl. Mix in the lard with your fingers until the flour resembles cornmeal. Add the water and mix until the dough comes together. Place on a lightly floured surface and knead a few minutes until smooth and elastic. Divide the dough into twenty-four equal pieces and roll each piece into a ball.

Preheat a large skillet over medium-high heat. Use a well-floured rolling pin to roll a dough ball into a thin, round tortilla. Place into the hot skillet, and cook until bubbly and golden. Flip and continue cooking until golden on the other side. Place the cooked tortilla in a tortilla warmer. Continue rolling and cooking the remaining dough.

Gran bundled the burritos in foil and flour sack towels, then packed them like sardines into insulated lunch bags to keep them warm. Sometimes Stella would slip in a handwritten note on a paper napkin telling Esperanza how much she loved her. It was a harmonious routine. Three generations of Gonzalez women with clearly established roles and a quiet respect for one another.

The Centre was crowded with other back-to-school school shoppers. They went straight to Target.

"Why do you need *those* jeans?" Stella asked as they stood in the fluorescent-lit dressing room. She held up a generic brand for half the cost. "These are just as nice."

"Mama, those are so ugly. I would *never* wear those," Esperanza said, wrinkling her nose. "These are what everyone wears. I have money from babysitting last weekend."

At five feet five inches and growing, she had recently surpassed Stella in height. She snuggled up to Stella.

"*Pleeeease,* Mama, please?"

"But they have rips in them! I'd have to mend them before you put them on for the first time."

"They're *supposed* to look that way."

Stella knew Esperanza would leave the generic ones hanging in her closet. There was no point wasting the money. She agreed and absorbed the happiness in Esperanza's face, smiling as she watched her daughter jump up and down and clap. Worth every penny.

"*Gracias,* Mama! Let's go to dinner at the food court."

The food court was crowded and noisy, but they found an open table in between McDonald's and Super Taqueria.

"What do you want?" Esperanza asked.

"I don't care. You choose."

"I'll get two orders of flautas. Save a table and watch our bags."

Stella's favorite time was when it was just the two of them, without girlfriends or a boyfriend there to divert her attention. She missed the days when she was everything to Esperanza. She knew it was natural for a seventeen-year-old to become more independent and find her own friends, but she didn't have to like it.

Esperanza paid for the flautas and carried them back to the table where Stella sat.

"For you!"

Esperanza held out the small cardboard tray of flautas.

"*Gracias, mija.* They look delicious."

Esperanza picked up one of the flautas, dipped it into the small container of guacamole, and crunched a bite.

"Did you hear about Ana Navarro?"

"No, what about her?"

"She tried to commit suicide again."

"What? Oh no. Poor girl. Is she all right?"

"She's in the hospital. She parked her parents' car in their garage with the door shut and ran the engine to poison herself."

"That's awful," Stella said. "Why would she do that?"

"She's always depressed. She cuts herself and wears all black. Says her parents fight too much and her father drinks and hits her mother until he passes out every night. I don't think she has any hope. Then she found out her boyfriend was cheating on her, and she just stopped talking to any of us. I haven't seen her at school for, like, two weeks." Esperanza devoured her flauta while she spoke and picked up a second one. Stella listened, sipping a Diet Coke.

"*Dios mío!* I hope she is all right and gets some help."

"The school has started coaching parents on the signs of teenage depression, sending home educational materials in English and Spanish," Esperanza said. "You don't need to worry about me though."

"I hope not. You would tell me if anything was wrong, wouldn't you?"

"You and Gran know everything about me."

Latina students were on the radar of school counselors. School psychologists called it a "high-risk time"—when young women from immigrant families tried to juggle expectations of teachers, friends, boyfriends, parents, and often grandparents simultaneously. Many were in foster care or trying to extricate themselves from gangs.

"*Tristeza*," Stella said, slowly shaking her head from side to side.

"*Tristeza?*" Esperanza wiped salsa from the corner of her mouth.

"Sadness," Stella said. "Ana's life is filled with sadness. Poor girl."

"That's for sure. She should have never slept with her boyfriend. That's when he started ignoring her."

Stella nodded, hoping Esperanza was learning from her friends.

Esperanza abruptly changed the subject.

"Why did you have to name me Esperanza? It sounds like an old Mexican lady's name." She slurped her Diet Coke.

"Esperanza is a beautiful name, *mija*. You are my joy. *My hope*."

"I still think it sounds like an old lady's name. But I guess old ladies aren't so bad. Gran is chill. Why did she name you Stella?"

"My name was a mistake. Gran wanted to name me *Estrella*," Stella said. "It means 'star.' But the nurse at the hospital in Oaxaca left the R off my birth certificate so I became Estella, just like that. Stella for short."

"Really? Is that true?"

"*Sí*. You can ask Gran."

Esperanza cleared their table and picked up the bag with her new jeans. As she emptied the tray into a trash bin she noticed two young girls pointing at her mother's birthmark and giggling. She moved in front of them so Stella wouldn't see.

"Speaking of Gran, we better get home. She's probably waiting for us," Stella said.

CHAPTER 9

Tony clambered in on the passenger side as Roger loaded his clubs into the backseat of his 2006 Porsche Carrera.

Roger slid into the driver's seat, cranked up the AC, and turned on his Bluetooth to take a call from Sheila Connors, a partner with the San Francisco law firm he depended on for all his business transactions.

"This is Roger."

"Hi, Roger. It's Sheila. We need to discuss these latest demands from Garvey."

Green Earth Organics was Sheila's biggest client. At eight hundred dollars per hour, she was happy to draft as many contracts as Roger needed. GEO's business helped make her one of the firm's superstars. Between drafting contracts with growers and putting together proposed mergers, Sheila logged more billable hours than the firm's IPO and high-net-worth divorce specialists. He relied on her advice for everything from reviewing indemnification clauses with grocery chains to helping with his estate planning. They were discussing GEO's latest contract, an agreement with another Salinas Valley grower to provide the bulk of next season's romaine supply.

"Just remember, you're swimming with the sharks now," Sheila said. "They may be farmers, but that doesn't mean they're stupid."

"It's a mute point. They have the land, and that's what we want."

"You mean *moot*."

"What?"

"It's a *moot* point Roger, not *mute*. *Moot* means of little or no significance. *Mute* means unable to speak."

"Whatever. You know what I mean."

Roger disregarded her warning. He knew they were sharks but would never concede they were smarter than him or Kate. His exit strategy was to use them for their land, pay them a minimal premium for growing organic, bank the majority of the revenues and sell the company for a hefty profit or take it public in a windfall IPO, all by the time he was fifty.

"I'm going to retire young and buy myself a little vineyard in Napa, maybe open a boutique investment firm and start playing with OPM, other people's money. No need to put my own chips in the game," he said. Roger didn't know anything about making wine, except that talking about it was impressive to young sales associates. And putting away a few bottles at dinner relaxed impressionable female staffers who eventually let their guard down.

"I expect an invitation to the first crush."

"You've got it. Entering a drop zone. I'll call you tomorrow."

He disconnected the Bluetooth and sped north along Highway 101 back to the office. Tony watched as they drove by miles of lettuce plants along both sides of the freeway.

"Who owns all this ground?"

"Not us. And they're converting more of it to organic every day."

Every farmer in the valley was getting in on organic, increasing supply and lowering the price. GEO's niche was fast becoming a commodity in an industry where brand loyalty was tough to build. Unlike the latest designer handbag, consumers didn't try to impress one another with name-brand lettuce. Roger's plan was to expand their product lines to make the company more attractive to potential investors. He was confident he could get $900 million, maybe even a billion, if the market continued to soar. He watched private equity cash flowing in Silicon Valley and the housing market booming. Money was cheap. Investors would get in a bidding war over GEO. They were, after all, producing and selling like never before.

Roger sped up to the security guard shack, stopped abruptly, and smiled at the blonde woman on duty.

"Hi, Karen. Hot enough for you?" Roger smirked.

She laughed uncomfortably. Roger could never just check in. He always had to flirt.

"Hi, Roger. Tony. How are you?"

"Doing well, thanks. Looks like lots of truck traffic here today."

"Yep, we're at full capacity. Don't worry, we're keeping them all in line."

"Good, that's what I like to hear." He gave her a wink and sped into his reserved parking space next to the main office's front door. The Porsche ticked as it cooled. The heat rolled off the asphalt in waves.

The record-breaking temperatures were making the news. For the past month, GEO was running at full capacity to package as much product as possible before the summer heat ruined it. With thirty processing lines running, workers stuffed as many leaves into the flumes as possible.

The receptionists were fielding a flurry of incoming calls on the switchboard as Roger passed the front desk.

"Call for you on line one, Roger," the receptionist said as he passed her desk.

He took the stairs two at a time toward his office and hit the speaker button as he sat down.

"This is Mark Manusco from the California Department of Health Services, CDHS. Is this Roger Worthington?"

"Hi Mark. Yes, this is Roger."

"I'm calling to inform you of a conference call tomorrow morning with the FDA regarding early statistical analysis suggesting that bagged salads are the source of a growing national E. coli outbreak. Several brands have been implicated, but they're being traced to a single plant in Las Flores, California."

"What brands are you looking at?" Roger asked.

"The one that links all cases so far is organic spinach, packed by Green Earth Organics."

CHAPTER 10

Cedar Rapids, Iowa

The Malmquist family phone tree was alive and well. Within an hour, grandparents, aunts, uncles, and friends from their church knew Bucky was in the hospital. Ruth was relieved to see Scott and her mother walk into the emergency room as she filled out pages of admitting paperwork. Brady ran to Scott, and he scooped him up.

"Daddy!"

"Hey there, little buddy! I hear your brother's not feeling so good."

"Yeah, he pooped all over the bathroom!" Brady said.

Juggling the baby and a clipboard, Ruth unhooked the BabyBjörn carrier and handed Brianna to her mother so she could focus on the approaching doctor.

Deep breath. Be strong.

Dr. Ryan looked more like a grad student than the head of pediatrics. His freckled face was friendly and confident. He motioned for Ruth to sit down and started flipping through the pages on his clipboard.

"There is a slight elevation in Bucky's white blood cell count." That's a sign that his body is fighting off an infection. His stool culture was negative for Clostridium difficile toxins, one potential cause of the diarrhea. We're still testing for Shiga toxin-producing E. coli. I'm going to put him on sulfasalazine to prevent more diarrhea," he said.

"What's that?" Ruth asked. "I'm suspicious of pharmaceutical companies and all the long drug names I can't pronounce. We don't use a lot of those pills at home. I'm not sure he's ever even had cough syrup."

"It's an anti-inflammatory used to treat ulcerative colitis."

"Ulcerative colitis? What are the side effects? He's only five and barely weighs forty pounds," Ruth said.

"It's a form of inflammatory bowel disease and could cause ulcers in the lining of the rectum and colon. I understand your concern, Ruth, but I don't want his condition to worsen, and we need to keep fluids in his body to reduce the risk of colitis. We monitor the dosage according to his age and weight, so you need not worry about it being too strong. I need to ask you a few questions about his diet too. Can you tell me what he's eaten in the past seventy-two hours?"

"Just our normal cereals, fruits, and vegetables. We ate chicken for dinner last night. Today we had Cherrios and smoothies at breakfast."

He scribbled onto his clipboard, nodding.

"Have you been out to a restaurant? Attended any sort of potluck or other large gathering with food? What about hamburger? Have you eaten any ground beef?"

"No. We rarely go to restaurants with the children, and we haven't been to any potlucks recently. No hamburgers recently either."

"What about any contact with animals? Have you been to a petting zoo or the county fair where he would have been in close contact with any livestock? Goats, pigs, or calves?"

"No."

He made some more notes in Bucky's file and then handed her another clipboard.

"We'll need you to fill out this form. It lists every meal, so we can get a clear picture of what he's eaten. Pay special attention to any ground beef, peanut butter, and leafy greens."

"Sure," Ruth said. She took the clipboard and looked it over.

"Be sure to list everything," Dr. Ryan said.

"I make smoothies with apple juice, bananas, blueberries, yogurt, and spinach."

"Did you wash all the fruit first?"

"Always."

"Where did the spinach come from?"

"I use the prewashed bagged mix we have in the refrigerator. It's organic. Green Earth or something like that."

"It's important to be as specific as possible, Ruth. We'll take a look at the completed forms and begin comparing that with what we've heard from other patients. Our first priority is to get Bucky healthy. If you have the packaging and receipts from your groceries, you should keep them all. We'll need to turn them over to County Health so the source can be traced."

CHAPTER 11

Stella and Esperanza walked into their cramped kitchen to find Gran sitting in her usual spot watching *Dancing with the Stars* reruns, her attention divided between the television and a pile of green beans in a worn apron sagging between her knees.

The house was small but immaculate. Gran kept the 1950s-era sunshine-yellow linoleum scrubbed with Original Scent Pine-Sol. Pink and purple Little Mermaid sheets hung from tacks over the aluminum-framed windows, casting a kaleidoscope of color on the floor like a stained glass window. Decades of dust from the surrounding fields settled in the cracks between baseboards, but Gran swept constantly and never allowed the dirt to take over. Stella appreciated the privacy of having a house instead of an apartment and did everything she could to remain in her landlord's good graces.

Gran snapped the ends off the beans and tossed each one into a pot filled with water. Tan support hose stretched across her fat ankles that bulged out the tops of a worn pair of black Famolares.

"I can't tell who I like better, Michael or Bruno. They're both gorgeous!" Gran said. "Where have you been? I see shopping bags."

"Mama took me to The Centre after school. I did good on my test, and the volleyball coach told me I'm going to be the starter!"

"Ah, smart girl!"

Gran picked a few wayward green bean ends off the table and added them to the discard pile.

"Esperanza, would you finish these *ejotes* for me? I want to talk to your mama."

47

Gran turned to Stella and motioned for her to come into the bedroom. She stood with effort, one hand on the table for support and the other gathering the apron full of beans. Stella followed Gran into the tiny room off the kitchen. Gran pulled the door shut so Esperanza couldn't hear them.

"Emiliano Cayeros from your work came by again today. Second time this week."

Stella lifted a small wooden figurine from the bedside table, a beat-up thrift store find with water-ring stains on the mahogany veneer that split and curled along the edges. She held the figurine, a brightly painted armadillo, turning it over and over in her hand.

"What did he want?"

She rubbed the figurine with her thumb once or twice, distracted for a moment.

"How should I know? You think he is going to tell me he wants to sleep with my daughter? Who is he anyway?"

Stella put the armadillo back on the bedside table and crossed her arms.

"I work with him at GEO. He's another wash line manager, and he's as tired of the place as I am. He wants to form a union."

"*Sí*, a union with *you, mija*! You be careful around him. I don't trust him."

With stout, calloused fingers, Gran brushed aside wisps of gray hair that fell from her tight bun but continued to hold her daughter's gaze.

"Mama, you don't trust anyone. I am almost forty years old. I can take care of myself."

"You are still young, *mija*. I tell you, be careful."

Gran reached for her right hand and gave it a reassuring squeeze. Stella stuck out her neck and gave her mother an exaggerated grin.

"*Sí*, I will be *careful*."

Gran softened.

Stella was a survivor. She had been twelve when she came to the United States in 1980, crossing the border with her mother to join her father who'd left them behind to find work in California. Before they joined him in California, she would go for months without seeing him. He tried to come home for Christmas during a planting break in the fields but sometimes didn't have the funds to make the trip. Her father carved fantastical painted wooden figurines known as *alebrijes* in Oaxaca, but didn't earn enough to support them. He reluctantly joined the stream of others like him headed north to earn money following the crops: strawberries, lettuce, tomatoes, bell peppers, and onions.

The winter she turned three, he carved and painted a figurine for Stella—a brilliant armadillo with magenta front quarters speckled in tiny pink dots and a backside zigzagged in bright yellow, blue, and green. It had a long, tapered snout and an upright tail and little feet with sky-blue toenails. Stella treasured it, her connection to the father she dreamed about. She brought it with her when she came to the United States and kept it during every move.

"*Mi armadillo* will protect me," she said.

She had always dreamed of being the first in her family to go to college. Her sporadic schooling had continued as they moved with the crops. Her father died when she was sixteen, leaving her and Gran on their own. It was 1984 and she dropped out of school and went to work for a restaurant, busing tables and washing the linens in the back room. She had wanted to study and take a high school equivalency exam so she could go to community college, but life's responsibilities kept getting in the way. A three-month flirtation with a friend's brother resulted in pregnancy.

She named her daughter Esperanza to symbolize her hope for a better life. She felt the same powerful love and affection toward Esperanza that her own mother gave her. Ever since she had been old enough, Stella had earned her own way. Esperanza's needs became her own.

By 1992 GEO had come to town and was hiring hundreds of new employees. Stella was twenty-four and tired of dish washing at restaurants. She jumped at the chance to work a regular shift with health benefits. The job at GEO would be indoors, packing the fancy salads Stella saw on supermarket shelves.

The steady paycheck allowed Gran to stop working in the fields and take care of Esperanza while Stella went to work. They enrolled Esperanza in the local elementary school and found a simple house to rent. Stability, finally.

In many ways her work schedule was ideal. It gave Stella five months off to work other jobs and allowed her to spend more time with Esperanza. She worked odd jobs cleaning houses and landscaping, got paid under the table and qualified for SNAP benefits to buy groceries. During the off season, the state's monthly unemployment check helped pay the $600 a month rent on the 950-square-foot house they rented in Las Flores.

Gran took the armadillo from Stella's hands.

"Your father is smiling down on you. I thought GEO didn't allow unions?"

"That doesn't mean we can't form one. Corporations don't make all the rules; there are laws that protect us."

"But why would you want to form a union, *mija*? They take good care of you as it is. Leave well enough alone and don't be a troublemaker."

"They *used* to take good care of us. I had my review today. Fifteen years at that place and a tiny raise again, barely enough to cover gas, after telling us we made all of our targets. It can't hurt to consider a union. You know they gave *themselves* raises."

"Why do you need a raise? We have enough to pay the rent."

"We may have enough to pay the rent, but we don't have enough to send Esperanza to college. I don't even know how we'll pay the fees for her volleyball team. And we don't have enough to fix the car if it breaks. Why should I work so hard so other people can get rich? I don't mind working hard, but I should make more."

"But we aren't poor. We don't live in a grungy apartment or a labor camp," Gran said.

"And I don't want to. What if I don't get hired back? Or if our landlord sells this house? We have no safety net. I want Esperanza to have choices. Do you want her to work on the wash lines? Or in the fields, rounded up like cattle every morning and crowded onto a school bus with rattling porta-potties towed behind?"

"You always take care of yourself, *mija*, I know. But sometimes there are people you have no control over. What if he gets you in trouble at work? You could lose your job before you even form a union."

"Don't worry so much, Mama. Emiliano is on our side. I promise."

CHAPTER 12

GEO's annual earnings before interest, taxes, depreciation, and amortization—*EBITDA*—was a healthy $60 million and growing. Roger liked the measure because it reflected sales but ignored capital expenses, debt payments, and other pesky liabilities like unions or E. coli. Roger's plan was to increase the EBITDA by $10 million a year as he prepared for liquidity. His pitch to investors on the IPO roadshow was simple: *growth, growth, growth. Twenty percent. Year over year.* Hammer it home with every presentation, and private equity clones will surely fall over themselves wanting to get in on the action. Their wives could brag to their friends about owning an organic salad company, so much more palatable than Exxon stock. Taking GEO public was another option.

He closed his eyes and pictured gold-medal winning athletes on the Olympic stage, humbly bowing their heads as medals were draped around their necks. With the third inhalation, he envisioned the opening bell on the NYSE. There he'd stand, front and center, behind the white stone balustrade on the balcony of the trading floor, surrounded by his executive and legal teams, smiling and waving. *I wonder if it's a real bell or just a recording? Ten-nine-eight-seven-six-five-four-three-two ... one! Brrinnnggggg!* Exhale. *Aaaaaaahhhhh.* He savored the image of himself modestly accepting the adulation from throngs of cheering traders on the floor below while thousands of employees back in California followed on a live stream video, projected larger than life on a wall at the plant. GEO's logo would hang behind him for the world to see, confetti pouring down like snow. *Take that, Salinas old boys and Harvard MBA pricks. Let's see you take your companies public.*

He was definitely warming to this visioning exercise … on a bit of a roll, in fact. *Almost better than sex.* A knock on the door broke his concentration.

Roger fumbled, thumping his chair back upright. He looked up to see Jane standing in his doorway holding a piece of paper.

"What's up? I don't want any more bad news today."

He relaxed at the sight of her toned legs. She slid the printout from an e-mail toward him as he put his glasses on.

> **From:** anne.hastings@usbank.com
> **Sent:** Friday, August 29, 2008, 4:35 p.m.
> **To:** Caroline.Boyd@GEO.com
> **Cc:** rich.wilson@usbank.com; matthew.zelinski@usbank.com
> **Subject:** RE: US Bank—Printer Lease
>
> Caroline,
> Here are comments from our credit department regarding your application for a new printer lease:
>
> *According to our financing research team, Green Earth Organics is presently trying to sell a 70 percent equity interest in the company to a private equity firm under a purchase and recapitalization agreement. Historically, it has been very difficult to get equity partners to stand behind a business by providing a corporate guarantee as well as a complete financial package for review. We would be willing to review a complete financial package in order to determine the feasibility of a guarantee.*
>
> *Your company is highly leveraged. Large amounts of goodwill and intangibles cause tangible net worth to be negative. The ratio of total liabilities to tangible net worth is 2.15:1.*
>
> *Your company also has a large amount of long-term debt with a balloon payment of more than $208 million coming due in 2010.*

In order to pursue your lease request we will need to mitigate these issues. After review, feel free to give me a call with any questions.

Regards,

Anne Hastings
Relationship Manager, US Bank
Machine Tool Finance Group
Phone: 800-636-0038
Fax: 415-831-2847
Cell: 415-936-5302
anne.hastings@usbank.com

Roger smacked the page down and glanced up sharply.

"What the hell is this? Where did you get this?"

"The bank sent it to Caroline last week when she inquired about a long-term lease for one of our printers in the marketing department."

"Who all has seen it?"

"Just Caroline and me."

"Good. Tell her to delete the e-mail immediately and ignore it. They don't know what the fuck they're talking about. What the hell do they think they're doing discussing financial issues with a marketing associate anyway? Christ. Over a fucking printer lease!" He looked disheveled and tired. "I'll take care of it from here."

Jane watched him ball the paper up and chuck it into the garbage can.

"What other bad news were you talking about?"

"I just got off the phone with Mark Manusco from the CDHS."

"And?"

"And it appears they've named us in a possible E.coli outbreak."

"What?"

"You heard me. E.coli. Outbreak. Green Earth Organics."

"What are the details? Why is he naming us?"

"I don't have details yet. He wants us to join a conference call tomorrow morning at seven a.m."

"Guess that means I'll hold off on announcing our expansion plans."

She handed him a draft press release.

> *Green Earth Organics is now growing its reach in grocery stores while investing in and expanding its pool of talented marketing professionals. With an ongoing commitment to launching new, healthy, and convenient products in the produce department and a new company initiative to launch new products in every aisle, GEO will add more than fifty positions to its team across the country. "We're investing in GEO's future by developing more convenient products and hiring our industry's top talent," said CEO Roger Worthington. "Our company's focus in 2009 is simple: develop innovative products with a focus on making organic food an easy and practical choice for all consumers."*

"Probably a good idea to hold off on this until we clear this up." He tossed the paper on his desk, shaking his head in disgust.

"Agreed. I'll notify the incident management team ASAP."

"I'd like everyone here at six a.m. to prep for the conference call," Roger said.

"Six it is," Jane said.

CHAPTER 13

Wednesday, September 3, 2008

GEO's chief financial officer Gregg Fluerant burst through Roger's door at six a.m. on Wednesday. He sat down in one of the two leather chairs opposite the desk next to Brendan Conley, chief operations officer in charge of food safety.

"How is our insurance coverage?" Roger asked before Gregg could start talking.

"We've got seventy-nine million dollars in product liability with AIG," Gregg said. "The proposal to increase it to one hundred and seventy-nine million dollars is sitting on your desk."

"Have we finalized it yet?" Roger asked.

"Nope. We were waiting for your signature."

"Shit."

Roger cupped his face in his hands. "And to think, I thought plastic packaging was going to be our biggest problem when we went on the IPO roadshow."

"We can manage this, Roger. It's not the first E. coli outbreak we've seen," Brendan said.

"Yeah, I know. But it's the first one that coincides with a potential sale."

Roger was too agitated to sit still. He rose from his chair and paced back and forth, shaking his head and running his hands through his thinning hair.

"Shit. Just as I was finalizing our exit strategy. Now we're going to have to wait until this blows over and pray there are no deaths to deal with. Kate is going to have a fucking conniption. I may be the first casualty of this outbreak."

He was as afraid of Kate's reaction as he was of what lay ahead with the FDA. He knew the unfolding scenario would require around the clock attention in the first days of the investigation. Her anxiety would only make things worse.

When Jane entered, Roger was in full crisis mode, working the phone and planning his response to the FDA.

"Shred everything from August fifteenth through twenty-ninth," he said to someone on the other end of the phone.

He cradled the phone's receiver and motioned for Jane to enter, mouthing the words, "Close the door."

"Who was that?" she asked while pulling the door shut. Roger slammed the phone down.

"Never mind about that right now. I need you to send Kate away for a few days."

She watched as he paced back and forth behind his desk. It was unusual to see him flustered.

"Are we really having people shred documents? Do you think that's a good idea?" Jane asked.

She looked at Brendan and Gregg, sitting in silence. The two of them shrugged, not willing to contradict Roger.

"Don't worry about the documents. I can't have Kate freaking out. I have to concentrate. You need to get her out of here, and it needs to be quick. Tell her—" He paused. "Tell her this trip was planned beforehand, as a surprise for her finishing her book or something. And then call the crisis management team together."

"Of course. I'll arrange for her to go to the Euclid."

The Euclid was the Worthingtons' favorite spa getaway, a retreat high in the Arizona desert where they attended various marriage counseling sessions and reconciliations over the years. Kate raved about it every time she came back.

"By the way, it's the *incident* management team, not crisis," Jane said. "IMT for short. We're having an *incident*, not a crisis. No need to propagate fear and panic."

"Whatever. You're the spin doctor, not me. The FDA is going to ask us to do a voluntary Class 1 recall."

"Voluntary?" Jane asked.

"What if we don't want to do a recall?" Brendan said.

"It's called voluntary, but they hold all the cards. Technically, they can't force us to do it, but if we don't they'll issue a statement nailing us, advising consumers not to buy Green Earth Organics. We need to send a letter to customers outlining steps we've taken to assure our products' safety. I'm not sure what to expect in these next few days. But I know I can't have Kate here."

"Does she know you're shredding documents?" Jane asked.

"It's just a precaution. We were front loading every line during August, and I don't think our production capacity needs to be scrutinized by federal investigators. Have you notified everyone on the *incident management team?*"

"Done," Jane said.

The incident management team included all department heads and Sheila Connors, patched in via conference call from San Francisco. A starfish-shaped speakerphone sat on the center of the long conference table. Everyone listened as investigators from the FDA in Washington, CDHS in Sacramento, and the CDC in Atlanta walked them through the status of the investigation. A quick round of introductions allowed participants to know who was on the call. Roger smirked when he heard several other Salinas Valley growers' names.

So it's not just us. This spinach could have come from anywhere.

The FDA investigator spoke first.

"Preliminary epidemiological evidence suggests that bagged, fresh spinach may be a possible cause of the outbreak. Several victims have reported consuming organic spinach, packaged at Green Earth Organic's manufacturing facility in Las Flores, California," he said. "Our team is in the air, on its way to California to begin their investigation. We are also ready to make an announcement about this, unless you agree to announce a recall. This is a nationwide public safety issue."

"What other brands have been implicated?" Roger asked. He wanted to hear the names of his competitors.

"The only common link at this time is Green Earth Organics," the investigator said. "We are looking into other people's purchases, but to date, Green Earth's spinach is the common link. We are advising that you initiate a voluntary Class 1 recall immediately."

The line was silent. Roger pictured his fellow CEOs, all within a forty-mile radius of GEO's offices, grinning, sitting in their own conference rooms. *Assholes.*

Options flashed through his brain like cards being shuffled in a dealer's hand. He scribbled on his notepad:

1. Reject the FDA's assertion that it was only Green Earth's brand.
2. Insist they finish conducting tests on the other samples before making a public announcement.
3. Go along with the Feds' demands.
4. Start making calls to highly paid, well-connected lobbyists in DC.
5. All of the above.

He circled number five. He was looking for resolution. He knew fighting the FDA would make GEO look guilty, as if they were trying to hide something or evade responsibility.

"What are the most recent illness reports?" Gregg Fluerant asked.

A new voice came through the speakerphone.

"This is the CDC. To date, fifty cases have been reported to us by county health departments, including eight cases of hemolytic-uremic syndrome, or HUS. One is reportedly in critical condition."

The room went quiet.

"Do we have details?" Roger asked.

"We think patient is in his or her eighties, but it's not confirmed.

HIPPA laws make getting details difficult. All we know is they're in Wisconsin."

"You're positive it's related to eating spinach?"

"There is a strong possibility. Patient was healthy and ate spinach two days before he or she got sick. The elderly and young children are the most at risk. States reporting illnesses include Connecticut, Iowa, Indiana, Michigan, New Mexico, Oregon, Utah, and Wisconsin. We expect these numbers to grow in coming days. We are scheduled to issue a press release in the next three hours warning people not to eat bagged spinach until we learn more."

Roger pressed the mute button on the speakerphone and turned to Jane.

"Draft a response stating that we are cooperating fully with federal authorities to find the source of the bacteria. Find the beef industry's most respected authority on O157. We'll need an epidemiologist and microbiologist on the crisis team, respected scientists who can build the case that this was an act of nature and could not have been avoided. Green Earth's processes are going to be scrutinized. We need to prepare for an onslaught of product liability cases."

Jane took notes as he spoke. Roger released the mute button and turned toward the speakerphone before continuing.

"Public safety is our first concern. We are the nation's largest organic salad company, and we will cooperate fully with this investigation."

"Sometimes being the largest isn't what you want," the investigator said flatly. "Kind of like tumors and waistlines: small is good."

"We take pride in making organic an option for all consumers," Roger shot back.

"That's all we have for today," the investigator said. "Our team is in the air and should be to your facilities by three o'clock this afternoon. We'll schedule another call for tomorrow morning, same time, to update you."

Gregg Fluerant clicked off the speakerphone and turned to Roger. "Next steps, Chief?"

"Let's break for ten minutes and then reconvene here to review our plan implementation and assign roles."

The group nodded in acknowledgment and then dispersed, subdued as a funeral procession.

During the A-shift morning break, lifers sat at the plastic Coleman picnic tables cramped in a trailer converted to a makeshift cafeteria. Lunch coolers were stuffed into small cubbies lining the walls. One window looked out on the parking lot. A soda machine hummed in the corner. The flat-screen television played a PowerPoint loop to keep employees informed on the latest company news. Slides included notices about GEO's new high deductible health plan and a cover photo of *Kate Worthington's Guide to Green Living*, where a smiling Kate stood out in a verdant lettuce field casually leaning on the handle of a hoe, sunlight reflecting off her henna-colored hair cascading around her shoulders.

Stella and Ofelia sat next to each other at their normal place in the middle of the room.

"I didn't know Kate was working in the fields now," Ofelia said.

The table erupted in laughter.

"All those foodies buy her book? Are they the same people who care so much about how their food is grown, if pesticides go in the soil, and how much sunshine a chicken gets? Why don't they think about how much sunshine we get? What about paying the people who wash their lettuce a living wage? They fight more for animals' rights than ours. I mean, I have nothing against chickens or anything, but they get more love than we do, and we're *people*! I don't get it."

"We're Mexicans," Stella deadpanned.

"Could be worse. At least we're not Mexican chickens," Ofelia said.

"It would be funny if it weren't true," Stella said. She unwrapped one of Gran's homemade burritos and took a bite.

"Mmmmm, I'm happy to have a Mexican *madre* make me this burrito every day."

Her coworkers nodded in agreement. A new slide appeared on the screen:

The Truth about Unions. GEO believes in maintaining an environment of open communication among all associates, both hourly and management. At GEO, we respect the individual rights of our associates and encourage everyone to express his/her ideas, suggestions, comments, or concerns.

Because we believe in maintaining an environment of open communication through the use of the open-door policy, we do not believe there is a need for third-party representation. It is our position every associate can speak for him/herself without having to pay his/her hard-earned money to a union in order to be listened to and have issues resolved.

Stella put her burrito down and addressed the other women at the table.

"Why shouldn't our daughters be able to go to college too? We work as hard as the sales reps, and in worse conditions. My car mileage isn't reimbursed. I don't get bonuses. If I don't do something, Esperanza will have my same fate," Stella said.

A few heads nodded in agreement. Ofelia and several others leaned in to hear more of what Stella was saying.

"Do you know how big the bonuses are in the sales department? I heard they equal our entire year's pay or more: fifteen thousand to two hundred fifty thousand dollars in *a single* check, given out every March. And for the company's top executives, bonuses are in the hundreds of thousands of dollars, depending on how many salad cases *we* packed and shipped!"

"That's just wrong," Ofelia said. "How do you know that?"

"Emiliano told me."

"Speak o' the devil."

Emiliano Cayeros walked into the trailer and reached for the chair beside Stella. He carried himself more like an owner than a line worker. At forty, he had twenty-five years of field and processing work under his belt. He was also an avid reader and loved books on business. Although he didn't have a college degree, he read enough to understand how business worked. He was a natural leader, self-confident and unconcerned about company policies banning union meetings. He listened at weekly meetings and shadowed his supervisors, taking in information like a nursing baby. He knew GEO's business model as well as Roger—maybe even better as someone working on the lines—and understood the company's thirst for agility and low-cost inputs.

"May I?" He pulled up a chair and turned it around, straddling the back of it with his legs and resting his forearms on the back.

"Of course," she said. Emiliano looked Stella straight in the eye.

"I came by your house yesterday."

"I know. My mother told me."

The other women grinned at Stella.

"Where were you?"

"Out."

"Next time I'll call first, but I didn't have your number and was in the neighborhood. I wanted to talk with you."

"About what? I've told you, I'm only interested in talking if you can promise I won't get fired."

"I don't give up that easily, Stella. Besides, I've told you, we're not doing anything wrong. They can't fire you. Do it for Esperanza," he said.

"What's *your* motivation?" Stella asked.

"*Justicia!*" he said. "I have no other reason."

She felt the other women watch for her reaction.

"I can't talk to you about this here."

He smiled, tilted his head back and gave her his signature chin point before handing her an empty bag of Doritos chips.

She looked inside to find a small handwritten note: *Emiliano: 901-2673*.

Unions were for major corporations who took advantage of their workers. Autoworkers in Detroit needed unions, not organic salad producers in California. Stella always assumed Kate and Roger ran GEO with her best interests in mind until she started talking to Emiliano. Maybe he was on to something.

He arranged for casual union updates to be held away from the lunchroom. He knew they risked retaliation if they got caught discussing it on company time. He also knew he needed to convince longtime GEO employees like Stella that union dues would be worth something. Employees heard of the abuses of unions from friends in the industry who saw dues deducted from their paychecks but saw little in return. Unions had lost the power and influence they enjoyed in the days of Cesar Chavez and earlier.

Stella's phone rang less than five minutes after Emiliano walked away. She looked down at her phone screen: *901-2673.*

"I knew it!" Ofelia said. "A booty call! In the middle of the day!"

"Mind your own business," Stella said as she flipped open her phone. "*Hola.*"

"Just come to learn about it. If you don't think it's a good idea, I won't keep asking you. I promise." He was out in the parking lot, looking in at her through the window.

"How did you get my number?"

"Your mother," he said.

There was a long pause. He waited.

"Okay," she said at last. "I'll go. For Esperanza."

"*Victory!*" He clapped his phone shut before she could ask any questions. Her phone chimed with a text message. *Details to follow.*

She smiled as she watched Emiliano throw a fist punch and click his two heels in the air.

Stella turned her attention back to the table where everyone was grinning at her.

"What are you looking at?" she said.

"You're blushing!" Ofelia said.

"Can we talk about something else?"

"Sure. I heard marketing got calls this week about a frog leg and a bloody Band-Aid in packages of spring mix, and yesterday some lady in Chicago reported finding an acrylic fingernail tip with a palm tree decal on it. I'm not sure what's worse, a dead frog or a body part."

"A nail tip is not actually a body part. It's not as bad as the finger," Stella said.

"I wonder what the marketing girls tell consumers who call in to complain? 'Sorry, we'll make sure to pay our line workers better so they don't have to use those cheap press-on nails anymore.' You think that's what they say?"

"We're supposed to be wearing gloves," Stella said.

"There was probably a hole in the glove. Haven't you noticed everything they use is cheap around here? Even the toilet paper gives me a rash!" Ofelia said.

Stella glanced at the clock and gathered her things.

"Back to the lines, girls. We don't want Pinocchio writing us up."

"You mean *feeling* us up. Keep us posted on Pretty Boy's plan to take over the world," Ofelia said.

CHAPTER 14

By Wednesday morning Bucky was surrounded by a team of nurses. Ruth stood in the corner of his room, helpless. One nurse pressed his forearm to find the best vein for a peripheral intravenous central line, a tube that would deliver life-saving fluids to him. He screamed as they poked and prodded him, writhing in pain and crying in spurts before calming down and moaning for Ruth to stay nearby.

After a long night, he had finally calmed down and slept for a full two hours. The room was dim and quiet except for the steady click of IVs delivering fluid and the rhythmic sounds of Ruth's breast pump. She was exhausted and took short naps in the chair next to his bed in between pumping milk into six-ounce bottles for Brianna. She labeled them with the date and put them in the small cooler she had brought to the hospital.

Dr. Ryan came in at 8:15 a.m. during his morning rounds. Ruth fastened her nursing bra and shirt before standing.

"Good morning, Ruth. Rough night?" he asked.

"I've had better. The chair actually isn't as uncomfortable as it looks." Ruth managed a smile, eager for information.

"Any test results back yet?" she asked.

"Not yet. We're giving him Vancomycin and Gentamicin, antibiotics to prevent bacterial peritonitis," Dr. Ryan said.

Ruth nodded. *More words I can't spell or pronounce.*

"We're also watching for a significant decline in red blood cell and platelet counts. If we see a decline, I'll order a transfusion with one hundred cc of packed red blood cells. We're monitoring for anemia and kidney function," he said.

"I can donate blood," Ruth offered.

"Actually, we don't advise that family members donate blood at this point," he said.

"Why not?"

"I have to be honest, Ruth. This could be a long and drawn-out recovery process. This is hard to hear, but if Bucky suddenly needs a kidney transplant, we'll need you to give blood then."

"A transplant?" she said, incredulous. "Oh my God." *From a stomachache to a transplant?*

"We are closely monitoring his kidney function and will continue giving him clear liquids. It appears his fluid intake is keeping up with losses. We will leave the IV access heparin locked for a repeat blood draw tomorrow. I'd like to move him to our pediatric care unit. It will be less hectic there."

"How long are we talking about?" Ruth asked.

She was getting used to the idea that this was more than a flu bug, but she was still unclear on whether the doctor was going to release Bucky. He kept prolonging a discharge with more tests and monitoring.

"It really depends on how he responds to treatment. It could be hours, days, weeks. I wish I could give you a definitive answer, but I can't until we know more. We've noted what he ate, and we're looking into a possible bacterial infection, which could lead to HUS. We've sent his stools into the lab to test for E. coli O157:H7. It's a nasty strain that can lead to some more serious problems."

"HUS?"

"Hemolytic-uremic syndrome. It's the abnormal premature destruction of red blood cells. If it's not treated, it can lead to kidney failure. We're going to have our lab run what we call a Sorbitol-MacConkey medium. It's a special culture plate they use to screen for E. coli O157:H7. We should know within twenty-four hours."

"You think he has food poisoning?" Ruth asked. "But I make all his food at home. We are very diligent about eating healthy foods."

"This is not your fault, Ruth. It could very well be related to a healthy food, but if it's contaminated with a pathogen, it still causes illness. Pathogens don't discriminate between restaurants and home-cooked meals, organic or nonorganic. They just look for the right conditions to multiply. A warm salad bag is perfect. It's like a little greenhouse for microbes. This is not a reflection on your cooking. We've seen several other patients reporting abdominal pain. The trend suggests a possible outbreak. We are in close contact with federal, state and county health officials who are keeping us apprised of any information they have."

"When will we know for sure?"

"We're running lab tests on his blood and stool samples, and we'd also like to test the spinach you used in the smoothies. Do you still have some in your refrigerator?"

"My mother is collecting the bags in our refrigerator. I'll have to go home and look. I don't usually save those kinds of things."

"Save everything: samples, receipts, packaging. These cases are built on evidence that the victim consumed a contaminated product. Produce bags have a production code on it that tells us exactly where and when it was packed. Do not throw it away."

"I think there was some left in the bag."

"Good. I'd like to keep him another night to monitor his fever and make sure his stools are solid before we send him home."

Ruth tried to hide her disappointment. She was hoping to bring Bucky home and cuddle with the other children together before bedtime. She tried to sound calm when she called home.

"I hope we'll be home tomorrow, boys. Bucky is doing better, and he can't wait to play with you in the backyard when he gets home. Be good for Grammy. I love you. Can you put her on the phone?"

Ruth took a deep breath, closed her eyes, and waited for Brady to hand the phone to her mother. *This will all be over soon. Our lives will get back to normal.*

"Ruth. How is he?"

"He's better, Mom. Dr. Ryan wants to keep him overnight just for observation, but his condition has stabilized, and we're hoping to bring him home soon."

"Oh, thank God."

"Please don't let the boys see you nervous. I don't want them to worry."

She looked down and rubbed her forehead, forcing herself to stay focused and not break down.

"We need to save the bag of spinach in our refrigerator. It's in the bottom left-hand produce drawer. Dr. Ryan may need it as evidence."

"Evidence of what?"

"I don't know, Mom. I'm just following his instructions. Apparently packaged spinach could be the cause of all this."

Ruth could hear her mother opening the refrigerator and fumbling for the bag. Sponge Bob's annoying giggle filled the background.

"Here it is. Green Earth Organics Spinach Mix. Is this it?"

"Yes. That's it."

"It says 'Use by August 29. Production code LF228A.'"

Ruth's heart sank. She continued in a calm voice.

"Do not use any more of that, Mom. Seal the bag inside another Ziploc bag. Dr. Ryan wants me to bring it in so they can test it for E. coli."

Bucky's nurse walked in the room looking down at her clipboard.

"I have to go, Mom. I'll call you later."

The nurse looked at Ruth and smiled. She was used to worried mothers.

"Hi. I'm Carla. I'll be the pediatric nurse on duty today. And who do we have here?" She smiled at Bucky.

"This is Bucky. I'm Ruth Malmquist, his mom."

"No need to worry, Mom. We'll take good care of him here. Dr. Ryan has ordered another round of tests. He wants to be sure Bucky's platelet count is not down and wants to check his white blood cells."

"How many more times are we going to have to take blood? Poor little thing must feel like a pincushion."

"We're looking for BUN, blood urea nitrogen. It's what forms when protein breaks down and lets us know if his kidneys are functioning properly. I know all of this is upsetting, Mrs. Malmquist, but it's better that we take precautions before his BUN levels get too high."

"Call me Ruth, please. Just do whatever you need to do to get him home."

CHAPTER 15

After the IMT meeting, Jane looked out the window of her first-floor office in Las Flores and watched truckers in the receiving area smoke, directly under the No Smoking sign, snuffing out their cigarette butts on the ground while they waited for their trailers to be loaded. She preferred the view of oak trees at her Santa Lucinda office. It wasn't enough that she had snagged a *Forbes* interview, helped Kate publish her book, and was working on the second. Now Kate wanted to be in *Fast Company*, on the cover no less. *Jeez.* She did her best to shake it off. It was hump day, after all. Investigators would be arriving in a few hours. She had to prepare for the mother of all audits. It wasn't even 9 a.m. yet.

Focus, Jane. The week is half over.

She had a 9:30 a.m. meeting with Caroline to firm up details for GEO's annual employee meeting and a 4 p.m. to review the *Forbes* talking points with Roger.

Caroline, already talking, knocked on the doorframe and walked toward her desk without waiting for a "Come in."

Full of ideas that one. Too many for her own good.

"Maybe we could have our employee meeting outdoors at the Roadside Stand this year? We'll need chairs for eight hundred, and a stage would be helpful to elevate Kate and Roger so they can speak to the crowd. We could use the meeting to debut our new products and give Kate a chance to talk about GEO's new green packaging strategy and product lines. I hear Costco can't keep the sliced apples on the shelf. We're beginning to feel some growing pains, so we want sales to be prepared with answers for customers about that. I've started hearing more and more complaints about all the plastic packaging. By the way, did you see Kate's response to my e-mail yesterday? Do you think I offended—" Jane stopped her midsentence. The girl was exhausting.

"Caroline, slow down. We need to focus and review costs before we turn this into a big party. You're all over the map. Kate already has an idea about what she wants to cover at the meeting."

"We can do whatever Kate wants. It's her company."

"We're thinking of asking a wash-line employee to talk about quality assurance. A lifer, someone whose seen our growth and is loyal to our mission."

"I think that's a great idea. Why didn't I think of that? I'll ask Maria Hernandez for a list of suggestions."

"Great. And yes, you did offend Kate, but I talked to her about it. Next time, don't be so eager to respond. Just wait until you have the answer and then reply. Here's my advice: only send e-mails that have useful information in them."

"I didn't realize being responsive was offensive."

Jane gave her an '*Are you serious?*' eyebrow raise.

"Caroline. Really? You know Kate doesn't like all the back-and-forth. If you don't have an answer for her, then don't respond until you do. Period. It's not complicated."

"Noted. Where should we plan for the meeting, here or at the Roadside Stand? I think the Roadside Stand would be prettier, but Las Flores is bigger."

"We can't do it at the Roadside Stand. There's too many people, and we have no way of getting them all there. We'll use the parking lot in Las Flores."

Despite the Roadside Stand's annual losses of $10 million per year, Kate had convinced Roger to keep it open as a marketing opportunity. Arranged more like a movie set than a farm, it was a perfect way to showcase GEO's history as a small, family owned farm to reporters and tourists. A full-time crew of eight kept the grounds meticulous for spontaneous photo shoots. They had planted an organic herb garden and built an outdoor entertaining area, complete with a redwood gazebo and professional kitchen for the occasional celebrity chef visit. It came in handy for personal parties too. Those who took a closer look knew there were two Green Earth Organics: the industrial factory in Las Flores and the idyllic family farm in Santa Lucinda. Different locations, different staff, and different Facebook pages.

Each fall the Roadside Stand's grounds crew planted a corn maze where local schoolchildren wandered to learn about organic farming methods. Soccer moms in Lululemon yoga pants sipped lattés and wove wreaths out of dried lavender. It was more than other salad companies did to educate students on the value of farming. Neighboring growers grumbled in local coffee shops about how their children came home from a field trip to GEO's Roadside Stand, asking their parents why they still used chemicals to farm.

Jane used it to host press visits, chef tours, and busloads of tourists wanting to connect with their food. Seasonal weekend workshops on garlic braids and pumpkin carving provided a convenient way to promote the GEO brand in the local media and interact with customers. A perfect response to all the "eat local" buzz. It was an effective marketing strategy, and one that competitors had begun to imitate. Jane never invited the public to Las Flores and rarely talked about manufacturing when interviewed.

The industrial side of food production is never as sexy as the farm. Plastic packaging was a growing public relations disaster. The irony wasn't lost on Jane. The very idea that put GEO on the map—bagged salad—had also become its biggest criticism as consumers began to shun excessive packaging. The company's annual donation to American Forests allowed GEO to point to how many trees they had planted whenever a reporter questioned their carbon footprint, but Jane knew the typical GEO consumer was smarter than that.

"Anything else, or are we done here?"

"There is one more thing, actually." Caroline shifted in her chair, trying not to look uncomfortable. "The Las Flores Women's Shelter is asking us for ten thousand dollars for their capital campaign."

"I'm not sure a women's shelter gives us the right kind of publicity.

We want people to associate Green Earth with health, not dysfunction," Jane said. She wanted Caroline to leave.

"I've heard that some of our employees have stayed at the shelter. It's the only one in Las Flores for victims of domestic abuse," Caroline continued.

"What I'm trying to say is, I'm just not sure they're in line with our *mission*, Caroline. We get a bigger bang for our buck if we sponsor *Sunset Magazine*'s annual Sustainable FoodFest. National media is there and Santa Lucinda's society set. Those expenses elevate our profile in the foodie community."

"Couldn't we do both? I think it's just as important to support the charities in our local community, don't you? The ones our employees actually benefit from?"

"I'd like to see what the ten grand will be used for. FoodFest's platinum tier sponsorship is twenty-five thousand dollars and gives us signage through the weekend, our own hospitality tent to grant media interviews in, and photos with Rick Bayless and Anthony Bourdain. Does the women's shelter do that?"

Caroline was beginning to irritate her. Jane had designed a multitiered approach to publicity with media articles, public appearances, and national awards. A low profile womens' shelter in Las Flores was not going to cut it.

"These national events are a must, Caroline. I'll ask Kate about the shelter donation and get back to you."

Caroline nodded and stood to leave.

"Do we know which employees have stayed at the shelter?" Jane asked.

"They don't give out names for privacy reasons, but she assured me our employees use it."

"I'll talk to Kate."

She still had to plan the Euclid getaway. She knew Kate would resist. She opened her e-mail and saw a message from Roger at the top of her inbox.

I've already called K with the news that the FDA is on its way and that investigation of our processes will be taking up most of my time in the foreseeable future. Convinced her that staying out of the limelight was a much better PR strategy.—rw

Roger was right: the investigation would be less stressful without Kate around. She rang Kate in Santa Lucinda.

"Jane! Just the person I was hoping to hear from. Are there any updates?"

Jane could hear Kate pacing and envisioned her biting her fingernail.

"We're still waiting for the FDA to get here, but you need not worry about that, Kate. I'm calling with the details of your trip. You deserve some time off," Jane said.

Her voice was calm and reassuring. Her first task was to get Kate out of the public eye.

"Enjoy your surprise. Really. Go to Arizona and think about how much you've accomplished with the book and the business and where you want to be in five years. Roger's on top of the outbreak situation. Everything will be okay."

"I'm not alone. We've built a strong team. Trust me, we do not want your face associated with an E. coli outbreak. Plain and simple. You are the face of healthy living and organics. You *know* that. The title of your book is *Kate Worthington's Guide to Green Living*. I can already hear the snarky comments from our competitors about how Green Earth Organics is killing people. We need to keep you as far away from this as possible. I can handle the messaging. We've brought in Hill and Knowlton in San Francisco to assist. They're pros. I've already arranged for your flight and made reservations at the Euclid. The plane leaves first thing Friday morning. That gives you a full two days to pack. Wheels up at six a.m."

To Jane's surprise, Kate didn't put up much of a fight.

"You're right. I know you're right. It's just going to be hard to watch from the sidelines, that's all."

Kate hung up before Jane could say anything else.

CHAPTER 16

The Las Flores facility received millions of pounds of raw product every day. Salad greens were washed, dried, and packed within hours of arrival on the backs of trucks coming from the surrounding fields. The delicate leaves were dumped from large plastic bins into pools of chlorinated water, swished around, and then put on conveyer belts where they moved uphill, meandering high above the floors through turns in the flumes like an amusement park log ride. Then they dropped forty feet down the waterslide to be rinsed in large pools below.

Stella and Ofelia sorted leaves for packing while debating the pros and cons of a union.

"I keep telling Emiliano not to ask for too much. Let's not get crazy. We'd be happy with a raise. First things first. This isn't Buckingham Palace. We're on the floor of a manufacturing company. Emiliano says this whole process works like a well-orchestrated symphony. If only the second violinists were appreciated by Roger we would have a beautiful concert. They are crucial to the overall sound."

Ofelia rolled her eyes.

"We don't have time for Pretty Boy's poetic comparisons. Just tell us what we need to do to pass a vote in favor of a pay raise before Pinocchio walks over here and hears what we're talking about."

"When they see our happiness has a direct correlation to production, they will have no option but to accept a union."

"And pay us more?"

"Yes. That's the union message to our coworkers *and* the owners. I'm going to help Emiliano distribute authorization cards and will need your help collecting signatures, out of sight from supervisors. All we need is a simple majority to move forward."

"What happens after that?"

"If we get a majority of votes in favor of a union, then we go to management and demand recognition as a bargaining unit, collectively, instead of them taking us one by one into Maria Hernandez's office and giving us no raises."

A supervisor approached them.

"I think that's enough union talk for now."

Ofelia motioned to Stella to change the subject.

"What time are you off today?"

"Same as usual, three p.m. I want to go to Esperanza's first volleyball game and check out the new boy she is seeing."

"Esperanza is a good girl, Stella. You don't have to worry about her."

"I want to keep it that way. He seems like a nice boy, but you know boys."

"You better get used to that, with her looks! She is going to attract every boy in the neighborhood."

"She already has. It makes me uncomfortable when she spends time with someone I don't know."

"Is he older?"

Ofelia was older and wiser than Stella. By age forty-nine, she had raised five children and knew the dynamics of teenage relationships. Her own daughter had given birth at eighteen but had stayed in an independent learning program at the high school. She'd graduated on time by taking an equivalency exam. Ofelia never bragged about her children, but she carried a silent, inner pride.

"Yes, I think he is eighteen or nineteen. His name is Raul Estrada. Esperanza doesn't give me many details, and she gets annoyed when I ask too many questions. I trust her, but I don't know him. He seems to come from a good family, from Durango, and I've seen him hold the door for her. I just don't want her getting in over her head. Her father is not around to intimidate her boyfriends."

"I'd send Bobby over, but I'm afraid they would just end up kicking back on your front porch and having a beer."

She and Bobby had been together thirty-two years and counting.

Ofelia's face looked weathered next to Stella's smooth complexion. A gold crown on her left incisor tooth sparkled as she talked. Like Stella, she was stout with dark-brown eyes and hair that she wore pulled back under her bump cap. They lived month to month, with Bobby spending precious paychecks on beer and picking up handyman jobs here and there. Her life was not as simple as Stella's, but so many moving parts created a chaotic joy that she thrived on. Their house was regularly filled with people, and there was always something cooking on the stovetop. Her children and their friends came and went in a steady flow, many considering it a second home. Esperanza was like another daughter to Ofelia. Hers was the house where the neighborhood children went for a meal or just to sit around and shoot the breeze.

"Thank you, Offie. I'll let you know if I need him."

"Don't hesitate!"

Ofelia put her arm around Stella, her eyebrows raised, and whispered in her ear. "You know Raul only has one thing on his mind, right? It's all any of them ever think about. We're all just products of some guy's ejaculation."

"Stop it!" Stella hit her friend on the shoulder. Ofelia laughed as she took off her bump cap and ran her fingers through her black, wavy hair.

"It's true! All of us are walking evidence of a male orgasm. No one ever knows if the woman enjoyed it, but none of us would be here if a man didn't have fun!"

She gestured her hands on either side of her crotch and pointed them upward.

"That's gross. Don't be so crude. Raul is not like that!"

"I'm just sayin'. Look, here comes one now: a walking erection waiting to find a parking place. And he's looking right at you. Pretty Boy. Mr. United Food and Commercial Workers himself," Ofelia said, grinning ear to ear as she nodded toward the door.

Emiliano motioned to Stella to get her attention, making eye contact and nodding his head backward to point at her with his chin. Stella liked that he noticed her. He looked directly at Stella, ignoring Ofelia.

"Hello, ladies."

"What did I tell you?" Ofelia said.

"Mind your own business, Offie," Stella said.

Emiliano handed Stella a card that read, in both English and Spanish:

> "*I hereby authorize the* UNITED FOOD AND COMMERCIAL WORKERS INTERNATIONAL UNION, *Local 5, chartered by the* UNITED FOOD AND COMMERCIAL WORKERS INTERNATIONAL UNION, AFL-CIO, *to represent me as my collective bargaining agent with my employer concerning wages, hours, and other conditions of my employment.*"
>
> *Print Name:* _____
> *Signature:* _____

"They'll punish you if they find out," Ofelia said.

"They won't know who is involved," Stella said. "If we don't do something, Esperanza will be standing on this same line in fifteen years. Is that what you want?"

"No. I'm just sayin' You should not be handing those out here."

"They don't monitor our every move. The meetings just look like tailgates. Besides, all of the security guards are gringos. They don't speak Spanish, so they have no idea what we're talking about."

"What are we going to get for the money they take from our checks?" Ofelia asked.

"They say we'll get automatic raises every year, better health insurance, and they'll be required to hire us back first when the season starts up again," Stella said.

"But they already hire us back every year," Ofelia said.

"Well, they've done it so far, but they don't have to," Stella said. "It would be nice to know that I'll have a job to help pay for Esperanza's college. When was the last time you got a raise? I know the office workers get raises every year. I don't know about you, but I have not been able to save anything. If I lose this job, I don't know what I would do."

Before her break, Stella slid her punch card through the slot of the electronic wall clock and walked toward Emiliano, who was standing with a group at his car.

"It will just take five minutes," he said.

She knew Emiliano was right about the need for a change. Her bills were mounting. Gran needed medication. Esperanza needed a new volleyball uniform. Gasoline was more than four dollars a gallon.

"I'm paying ninety-two dollars a month for health insurance. I could be saving that for Esperanza's college. Can you change that?"

"*Sí.*" He flashed a wide smile at her.

"I only have ten minutes," Stella said.

"We'll be done in less than nine, I promise. If we can get fifty percent of us to sign the union authorization cards, GEO would have no choice but to negotiate. Until now, management has convinced us we are treated well. But that's not true."

"I've heard rumors we're being investigated for an E. coli outbreak," Stella said. "How is that going to affect people's appetite to form a union when our jobs may be at risk anyway?"

Emiliano leaned in, out of sight of the security guards and cameras.

"A product recall is just another distraction. We lifers are *waaaay* down the list of priorities. We come after Roger's family, his growers, his lawyers, and his sales staff. With a union, he will finally have to pay attention to the people who earn his money. We will collect the cards next week. Everyone needs to encourage one another to sign. That's all you have to do, and we'll take care of the rest."

She agreed to spread the word quietly. As she walked to her car, she noticed the security guard with a clipboard writing down the names of all the employees who had stayed for the tailgate.

They can't punish me for talking to friends during a break. Nothing illegal about that.

CHAPTER 17

Between meetings, Jane was reviewing the wording on a letter to customers about the recall when her phone buzzed.

"They're here," the receptionist said over her speaker phone.

"I'll be right out."

She called Roger to alert him and sent a quick group e-mail to the incident management team to meet in the executive conference room in ten minutes. She took a deep breath and pulled out the mirror she kept in her desk drawer. She applied some clear lip gloss and checked for food in her teeth.

Here we go. It's show time.

The FDA inspector, Emily Putnam, was all business. She had taken a morning flight from Washington, DC, and drove straight to Las Flores from the airport. Her colleague, Jerry Halperin, was from the CDHS. He had driven two hours from Sacramento to meet her in Las Flores.

Jane greeted them at the reception desk.

"We'd like to start with interviews of your department heads," Emily said. "And then we'll need to tour the plant."

"Of course," Jane said. "Can I get you some coffee or tea? You must be tired from your flight."

Emily made it clear from the start that this would not be a social visit.

"No, thank you. I'm fine."

Roger met them in the conference room with a cordial hand shake and his usual confidence.

"We're here to assist you in any way we can," he said. "I've directed my department heads to cooperate fully and provide you with all the documentation you request."

"We appreciate that," Jerry said. "We'll begin with individual interviews, one-on-ones."

"Okay," Roger said. "Feels more like an interrogation than an interview."

Emily and Jerry were stone faced.

"We're just following protocol," Emily said.

They spent three hours interviewing Gregg Fluerant, Brendan Conley, and Roger, collecting records and taking notes. The afternoon was a flurry of back-and-forth phone calls with Sheila Connors in San Francisco, approving which documents they could hand over, public relations executives at Hill and Knowlton approving the wording of letters to customers, and a press release for the public.

CDHS requested to approve all communications regarding the outbreak. Jane was fielding calls from panicked attorneys for the insurance company and customers asking if it was safe to eat GEO's bagged salads.

She reserved a conference room to make room for the growing file requests from Emily and Jerry: production logs, employee handbooks, standard operating procedures, previous safety violation notices, sanitation logs, employee sick day records, organic certification audits, grower contracts, and copies of every e-mail sent in the past six months. Sheila Connors instructed her to make copies of everything and document what was being turned over to investigators.

"We'll have to redact any information that falls under GEO's proprietary information," Sheila told her. "We'll need to approve every document handed over."

Jane pictured Kate choosing which bathing suit to pack for Arizona, while she fielded calls from five reporters looking for a comment. Her office turned into the situation room, where they discussed strategy and next steps as federal investigators zeroed in on GEO as the single source and main culprit of what was growing into one of the largest and deadliest foodborne illness outbreaks in history.

Calls from CBS, NPR, and the Associated Press piled up in her voicemail. Reporters wanted a comment on what GEO was doing to ensure the safety of its products and what they would do to help victims.

After the one-on-one interviews, Emily and Jerry toured the facility, taking water and temperature samples from the wash lines. They told Jane they would return the next morning with their environmental specialist team for more testing and document collection.

When they left Jane collapsed in her chair and looked at the clock on her wall: 10 p.m.

They don't call it hump day for nothing.

CHAPTER 18

Thursday, September 4, 2008

The following morning, Jane went to her Santa Lucinda office to update Kate and assure her everything would be fine while she was gone.

Wheels up at 6:00 a.m. tomorrow.

Kate was sitting in her office when Jane walked in.

"About today's conference call," Jane said. "Here's the number. You can call in, but I don't recommend it. You should be packing for your trip. We expect the FDA will publicly name Green Earth Organics as the brand that has caused people to get sick, but we have a response ready to go."

"Aren't there others involved?" Kate asked.

"No, at least not yet. They say the number of illnesses being reported is increasing though, so there may be more. We're working to draft talking points, and I will keep a strict policy on who talks to the media."

"Are they linking it to organics?"

"Not necessarily. They're still investigating. This could have a negative effect on your book sales, though. We need to distance you from the entire situation."

"I know. You're right. I really shouldn't be anywhere near this mess. I knew we shouldn't have packed the wash lines so full. I warned Roger about this. He directed Brendan to process too much, too quickly. The sales targets are unrealistic. All to impress potential buyers, and now look at the mess we're in."

Jane was running interference between Kate and Roger, trying desperately to have Kate leave on a calm note. She stood on the opposite side of Kate's desk eager to get through her checklist of priorities for the morning. The landmines were too many to count between Roger and Kate. She steered away from Kate's focus on the mistakes and turned to solutions.

My job is to find solutions.

"We've hired an outside firm to handle consumer calls. I want to be sure every call is answered by a real person and that our customers know how to dispose of products they may still have in their refrigerators," Jane said.

"Have we drafted a press release yet?" Kate asked.

"That's next on my list. FDA and CDHS both have to sign off on anything we send out. But you don't need to worry about any of that. I just need you to focus on which bathing suit you're going to pack for the Euclid."

"I'll take the time to start an outline for my next book. We're going to need some good press when this is all over."

"We'll take care of the employee meeting details while you're away. If anything comes up that I think you should know about I will call, but really you should just plan on being off the grid for a few days."

Kate was rearranging the photos on her desk and gathering a stack of papers to take with her.

"Oh, and I wanted to run a donation request by you. Caroline is asking us to consider a ten thousand dollar check for the Las Flores Women's Shelter. I told her I didn't think it was a big bang for our buck. Not really in line with our mission."

"Jane, don't be such a brown nose that you put GEO's interests before human beings. Our mission does not exclude the *people* who live on the earth, especially abused women. Give ten thousand dollars to the shelter and offer them a year's worth of free salads. They probably need the folic acid."

"Of course. Of course. I was just —"

"I know what you were doing. Putting GEO first. I appreciate that, but I think we're seeing the consequences of that, so let's try thinking beyond our mission statement for a change."

CHAPTER 19

Stella sat in her usual spot at the lunch table next to Ofelia and group of new recruits talking about working double shifts.

During August and September GEO ran two full shifts to pack all the orders. Workers bargained with each another for shifts. Those who wanted more hours traded with others who needed the time off. Young mothers with working husbands were always the first to ask for a shift swap. One of the women, Blanca, had signed up for back-to-back shifts, a common practice for new workers who had yet to realize the toll of a sixteen-hour day.

"My husband just got a job as a security guard, but his schedule was shifted yesterday without notice. I don't have anyone to watch the baby when he goes to work at night," Blanca said.

Stella didn't recognize her but could hear the angst in her voice. She remembered the days of juggling childcare, a job, and needy family members.

"I can work the B shift for you tonight if you need to stay home with the baby," Stella said.

Blanca turned to her, surprised.

"Really? You don't need to be home?"

"My mother is there. She can keep an eye on Esperanza," Stella said.

"It's just one night, and I'll work a shift for you sometime. I promise," Blanca said.

"No problem," Stella said. She knew the favor would never be returned, but she didn't care. It would be an opportunity to gather B shift workers' signatures and help a young mother at the same time. The

B shift started at 4:00 p.m., after a daily sanitation, and ran until all the cases on the schedule were packed, usually about 1:00 a.m.

After the B shift Stella saw Emiliano motion for her to join a group of three others outside the back door. *How did he manage to be standing there at the end of every shift?* She grabbed her lunch from the cubby and slid her time card through the clock to sign out.

"Do you live here, Emi? Why are you working both shifts?"

"No, just tonight. I'm distributing more cards. It's up or down. All we need is a simple majority. It will need to happen quickly because we want to finish negotiations before the move to Yuma in November. If we get a majority of employees who want to pursue this, then they have to enter into talks," he said.

Emiliano knew the September push was the perfect time to capture employees' attention. The long hours and low paychecks annoyed people.

"How will we conduct the vote?" Stella said.

"We'll use the authorization cards I've been handing out. Employees just have to print and sign their name on the cards, and a few us will collect them. We'll count them and know that evening what the results are."

"I thought all votes were anonymous."

"Stella! Stop being so paranoid. How many times have I told you: they cannot punish you for talking about a union. This is America. We have rights."

"But others have told me we can get in trouble and that we shouldn't be having these meetings at all, especially not on-site. You have less at stake than some of us, Emiliano. I need this job to take care of my mother and daughter. And Esperanza wants to go to college. I can't afford to lose this job."

"They have no way to prove that you have been talking about a union. You have a right to gather with friends and talk, don't you?"

"I guess so."

She looked down at her feet, still unsure if she was doing the right thing. She felt like a traitor. GEO had taken care of her for so many years. It was a good job in comparison to other jobs she'd endured.

Stella took a stack of authorization cards from Emiliano and stuffed them in her jacket pocket before turning to walk to her car under the blue fluorescent lights of the parking lot. A fellow worker walked with her.

"Any news on the union?" he asked.

"Yeah. The more I learn, the more I think the union would be a good thing. A union would represent all of us as a block, rather than each of us having to represent ourselves. No more one-on-one closed-door sessions in the HR office. No more worrying about whether we'll be rehired next season. No more unpaid sick days or overtime or lunch hours cut short in order to fill special orders. No more three-year stretches without a cost of living increase or overpriced health plans."

"If it sounds too good to be true, it probably is," he said.

"Think about it. We would have so much more power if we worked together. They need us more than we need them," Stella said. "Management will finally have to recognize the contributions we make to the success of Green Earth." She handed him an authorization card.

"What do I do with this?"

"Read it and sign it. You can hand it to me or Emiliano tomorrow, but be discreet."

She unlocked her car and turned on the heater as soon as she turned the key. Her breath formed a cloud under the parking lot lights in the cold morning air.

By the time Stella got home at 2 a.m. Esperanza was asleep on the worn corduroy couch pushed up against the wall in the kitchen, a twenty-five-dollar garage sale find. A gold-and-orange crocheted blanket, usually draped over the top of the couch to hide a tear in the upholstery, was pulled over her. Esperanza's long legs stretched the length of the couch. She wore sweats, and her feet were covered with a pair of red socks worn by Las Flores High School's varsity volleyball players.

"*Mija*, you should be in your bed."

She touched Esperanza's ear as she brushed her daughter's long, brown hair away from her face and kissed her on the forehead. "You'll sleep better there."

"I was sleeping fine until you woke me up," Esperanza said.

"I don't like you watching so much television. Did you finish your homework?"

"Yes, Mama. I always finish my homework. I got an A on my algebra test, and a scout from Berkeley came and watched our volleyball game today."

"So smart. My sweet girl. Now get to bed."

Half-asleep, Esperanza shuffled the ten feet to her room, a former back porch converted to a bedroom. She climbed into her bed and fell back asleep. Stella kissed her again and walked down the narrow hallway. The white walls were lined with eleven eight-by-ten photos of Esperanza, one for each year since kindergarten, hung in cheap gold frames from Kmart.

Stella stepped into her own bedroom, peeled off the layers of heavy ski clothes down to her underwear, and looked at herself from the waist up in the mirror that hung above an old dresser. She climbed up on the foot of her bed to get a full view and turned to see her profile. She sucked her stomach in.

"Could be worse," she said.

Then she climbed into her bed, relieved to be off her feet and under her warm blankets. She drew the covers over her shoulders feeling a deep sense of gratitude for her daughter and mother. The balls of her feet ached from standing all night, and she could feel the calluses on her hand from holding the knife for so long.

Stella closed her eyes as sleep crept toward her. Memories of a young Esperanza flooded her mind. She saw her toddler running in the park. She used to watch her from the bench, thinking to herself what a gift God had given her: a beautiful, healthy, perfect daughter. Esperanza was Stella's mark on the world, her contribution to the community, and the only link continuing her parents' lineage beyond her own life. She didn't like to pressure Esperanza, but in Stella's mind, her daughter was everything. Stella used to comb her straight, brown hair into two neat braids tied with matching ribbons, which bounced when she ran. Esperanza's hair had grown long and more sensual as she got older, prompting second glances from men who walked by.

She'll have it better than me. Mi pequeño pájaro volará libre.

Stella thought of Emiliano's smile. She gave her wooden armadillo a kiss and fell asleep resolving to form a union.

She woke up a few hours later to Gran telling Esperanza to get up.

"Time to get up, *princesa*. The bus will be here in fifteen minutes."

"Oyyyyy, I don't wannnnna go to school today," Esperanza moaned into her pillow.

"You shouldn't stay up so late reading that damn cell phone till the sun comes up. How much does that cost anyway?"

"I pay for it with babysitting money, Gran. Don't worry."

Gran turned to walk back to the kitchen where she was warming fresh tortillas to put in Stella and Esperanza's lunches and watching the *Today* show. Esperanza dragged herself the five steps from her bedroom to the kitchen, looking disheveled in her sweatpants and tight T-shirt.

"Hmmm, look at that handsome Matt Lauer," Gran said. "He's talking about Las Flores!"

"What?" Esperanza said. "We're on the news?"

"*Sí*, something about an E. coli outbreak. Go wake up your mother, *hurry*!"

Stella could hear them from her room and sat up in her bed.

"Mama, come quick. GEO is on the *Today* show!"

She threw her robe on and joined them in the kitchen. The three of them huddled in front the clunky Zenith television on the kitchen table, another one of Gran's garage sale finds. Matt Lauer's familiar voice filled the room.

"One person has died and dozens of others have been sickened by a deadly E. coli outbreak believed to be caused by bagged spinach," Lauer said. "The FDA is warning consumers to throw out any bagged spinach packed by Green Earth Organics of Las Flores, California. Investigators at the CDC say there are reports of illnesses in several states, and that children under the age of three and the elderly should be especially cautious. For more information, consumers are asked to call the number on our screen."

"Someone died?" Stella said. She raised her hands up over her mouth and watched as the camera panned to an aerial photo of GEO's Las Flores facility. "That's us!" she said.

"That's what Matt said," Gran said. "And Matt knows everything."

PART II

Dreamers

CHAPTER 20

Friday, September 5, 2008

Kate parked her white Range Rover at the Santa Lucinda Airport, not much more than a private airstrip, and turned the engine off. It was still dark out at 5:45 a.m. She flipped on her visor light to scan the brochure Jane had slipped into her bag.

The Euclid's own Dr. Aurora Hukura possesses ten years of experience in naturopathic medicine and over twenty years of experience as a psychic and massage therapist. Her extensive qualifications allow her to practice and teach master-level deep tissue, structural massage, and spiritual healing. Areas of specialization include acupuncture, homeopathy, trauma therapy, and cranial sacral massage therapy.

Developed expressly by Dr. Hukura for the Euclid, the healing experience offered through our Spirit Flight package focuses on physical and spiritual consciousness. You will achieve a deep meditative state as balance is restored to your energy fields. This treatment combines a full-body therapeutic massage with the ceremonial and healing practices of spiritual Shamanism and drumming, while also employing acupuncture, cranial sacral therapy, and spinal alignment to renew your body's energy and balance. After your Spirit Flight massage and meditation, Dr. Hukura will meet with you one-on-one for a private reading of your future.

She needed some guidance on the direction of GEO and wanted the advice of someone on the outside.

GEO's pilot, Harry Vetterkind, greeted Kate in the parking lot. Harry was retired air force and still looked the part. Impeccably dressed with his starched white Polo shirt tucked into belted Dockers, he was James Bond meets Tom Cruise. His crew-cut hair complemented his tanned skin and aviator sunglasses, which were perfectly matched with a chocolate-brown leather bomber jacket.

Harry ensured that GEO's management team traveled back and forth from Las Flores to Yuma safely and in style. He also flew the Worthingtons on personal trips. He took great pride in keeping the plane immaculate and well stocked with an assortment of Evian and Perrier waters, organic juices, and Hansen's natural sodas. Depending on the passenger list, he stocked wine and beers with an assortment of candy bars and nuts. When Kate flew, he knew to have no candy onboard and alcohol only if she requested it. There would be no alcohol on this early morning flight. She wanted to get out of town before reporters started calling and be at the Euclid in time to have lunch poolside.

"Good morning, Kate," Harry said. "Right on time. We should be in Sedona by ten a.m."

He unloaded her Tumi luggage from the back of her SUV.

"Hi, Harry. How are you?" Kate smiled.

"Good. Off to Sedona for a little R&R?"

"Yes. It's been such a crazy year. Roger insisted I take some time away."

"You deserve it."

Harry represented escape. He carried her bags up the short staircase of the Piper M600. Freshly brewed coffee and an assortment of sliced strawberries, pineapple spears, and warm bran muffins awaited her. Flying on the company plane was like stepping into a serene bubble with butter-leather seats, new-smelling carpet, and varnished wooden sideboards.

"Jane requested Greek yogurt and fresh fruit, so it's all ready. Can I get you anything else before we take off?"

"No, thank you, Harry." She sat back in one of the plane's recliners and fastened her seat belt. Then she wrapped herself in a Frette cable-knit cashmere throw and closed her eyes.

Deep breath. Breathe in. Breathe out.

She loved watching the sun rise above the mountains of Santa Lucinda. It was such a relaxing and ethereal way to start the day.

She listened as Harry and his copilot performed the standard safety checks with the control tower. The plane turned and began its roll down the runway for takeoff, picking up speed as it propelled forward.

"Ten, nine, eight, seven, six, five, four, three, two, aaaand takeoff."

Concentrating on her breath and making an effort to relax, Kate closed her eyes and started to think about what she would accomplish in the next four days.

Deep breath. Transformative change.

She imagined herself on a beach, walking along the surf with the sun shining on her auburn hair.

The plane continued to climb, leaving a white tail behind it.

Deep breaths, Kate. Breathe in. Breathe out.

She pictured Roger at his desk on the phone with investigators desperately trying to salvage their future. She had to hand it to him—Roger had lived up to her expectations. She reclined her seat back farther, took another deep breath, and then exhaled slowly.

A pocket of turbulence dropped the plane a few feet, jolting her from her melancholy and making her heart pound.

Oh God, what if this plane goes down?

Harry's voice came through the intercom.

"Sorry about that, Kate. We're passing through a patch of unsettled air, so it may be choppy for a while. I'll adjust our altitude and see if I can get us out of it. Nothing to worry about though. The sky looks clear, and visibility is tip-top."

She relaxed a little and tried not to focus on work, but her thoughts kept returning to GEO. *New products. Expansion. IPO. Private equity.*

Liquidation. Exit strategy. Her head was spinning. Despite her millions, Kate still felt poor. The company had incurred so many expenses, and their debt nagged at her. Still, she was confident Roger would navigate them through this latest bump and have them coming out ahead. He always had before. The falling stock market was only making her more agitated about not selling before the outbreak.

She would relax this week and map out where she wanted to take GEO before they sold it. She was determined to make her exit smoothly and fold the past fifteen years neatly into the next chapter of her life. Before they sold, she would expand GEO's salad lines and develop new products like frozen fruits and nutrition drinks.

Upon arrival at the Euclid, Kate was ushered to her room by an attentive resort staffer. The room was fragrant with the smell of the fresh, white peonies arranged in a glass vase on the bedside table. An all-organic menu sat beside it.

After unpacking her yoga clothes and various bathing suits, she settled in and ordered a caprese salad with organic olive oil and basil, bottled Fiji water, and a smoked wild salmon fillet. Then she booked a yoga class, a massage, and an appointment with Aurora.

CHAPTER 21

Cedar Rapids, Iowa

Ruth awoke to bright sunlight peeking through the ugly peach curtains. She hated everything about the hospital: its dated decor, the smell of disinfectant, the constant comings and goings of different nurses to check Bucky's vital signs, and the gray, soggy food. She wanted homemade meatloaf and to cuddle in her own comfortable bed reading bedtime stories. It had been four days since they checked in to St. Luke's Hospital. She watched as he breathed calmly, hooked up to an IV machine and sleeping peacefully, a rare respite from the past ninety-six hours.

Dr. Ryan arrived early. Bucky was the first stop on his daily rounds. He looked somber, as if he too spent the night by his child's bedside.

"Good morning, Ruth. Did you get any sleep?"

"Not really. I'm still pumping milk for the baby. I just want to get Bucky home."

She held her breath, praying for good news. She didn't want to break her promise to Brady and Brian. She knew they would call her on it if Bucky didn't come home by the end of the week.

"We want him to go home too. Bucky's blood and urine tests revealed significant amounts of protein, a strong indication that he could be developing HUS."

"That leads to kidney failure?"

"Not necessarily. That's a worst-case scenario, but we can mitigate it until we get his kidney working again. The high protein means his kidneys are not functioning properly and that there is a risk of thrombocytopenia, or low blood platelet count. The tests are also showing higher levels of liver enzymes, indicating a number of possible complications."

"Like what?"

"We are doing our best, Ruth, but I have to be honest with you. This is a very serious situation. I've called in a social worker for you and Scott and a pediatric gastroenterologist for consultation. Bucky is in good hands here. We have a strong team of specialists, and we are in contact with experts around the country."

"Thank you, but I don't think we need a social worker. We have plenty of support."

"Even the healthiest families benefit from having a professional to talk to, Ruth. In just four days, Bucky's stomachache has transformed into a life-threatening emergency. There's nothing to be ashamed of in getting some help. There are coping strategies that will help you get through this."

"When will we know the cause? Do you think it was something he ate? Is it contagious? I'm worried because I gave the smoothies to all three boys, and I want to make sure they're not going to get sick too."

"We're awaiting the lab report from the bag of spinach you brought in. The county health department is communicating with the CDC to see if there's a connection between Bucky's illness and others we're seeing around the country. They will test the product that's left, and then we'll know whether or not it was contaminated."

"What should we do to protect the other children?"

"We know E.coli is highly contagious and could be airborne. Make sure no one eats anything from that bag. And you need to watch carefully that the other children are not developing similar symptoms: stomachaches, fever, diarrhea, anything out of the ordinary. E. coli O157:H7 is a mysterious pathogen. And young children and the elderly are the most susceptible."

Bucky moaned in pain. Ruth couldn't tell if it was all the medications and machines he was hooked up to or if he was still experiencing abdominal pain. The nurses told her he was probably having side effects from all the drugs.

She rubbed his arm and tried to sound cheery.

"I'm right here, sweetie. Don't worry, I'm right here." She wanted him to know she wouldn't leave his side.

When she realized his hospital stay would be longer than two days, Ruth had decorated his room with colorful scribbles from Brady and Brian. She made a little shrine on the windowsill with a cross and get-well notes from members of their church. Balloons and flowers from friends were bunched into a corner by the window. The LDS church sent cards and had started a meal calendar to help Scott. They couldn't have visitors due to the hospital's rules that limited people in the ICU. She watched as nurse after nurse came to take Bucky's blood pressure.

"Can't we do anything to make him more comfortable?"

"The PICC line should make blood draws less painful. It means we don't have to keep poking him with new needles," the nurse said matter-of-factly.

Ruth nodded politely.

"Thank you. He's only five."

"I know, Ruth. I know. Don't worry. He's in good hands here. I promise."

She nodded to be polite but knew that even the best doctors in the world couldn't save a child from kidney failure.

CHAPTER 22

Gran turned up the volume on the television while Stella and Esperanza stood, staring in silence at Matt Lauer.

"Are you going to lose your job, Mama?" Esperanza asked.

"No, of course not, *mija*." Stella was numb. *There goes the union vote.*

"I wonder who died," Gran said. "Did he give a name?"

"They're probably across the country," Stella said. "You know we ship our salads all over the place. I'm sure I'll find out more at work."

Stella was back at the plant in time for the A shift start at 8:00 a.m. The floor was abuzz with talk of the recall. As she walked toward the smock room, she saw one of the new HR specialists walking toward her. Her heart rate started to rise.

"Good morning, Stella," the girl said. "Would you mind stopping by the HR trailer before your shift this morning? Your supervisor knows, so don't worry about being late."

"Sure, what for?" Stella asked.

"Oh, it's nothing. We just wanted to ask you a few questions," she said.

She nodded, hands tucked into her jacket pocket.

A coworker walking with her leaned closer to Stella and whispered, "Are they going to ask you about the union?"

"I don't know," Stella said. "We'll find out, I guess."

She breathed in, trying to stay present and not let her worst thoughts get the best of her. *I still have my job. My supervisor knows I work hard. None of that has changed.*

Layoff and bankruptcy rumors were flying around the facility all morning, but none of the line workers were told about the FDA investigation. Federal and state investigators blended in with the regular food safety and organic certifiers. They carried clipboards and wore white bump caps with VISITOR printed above the visor.

Stella stepped into the bathroom before she went to the HR trailer. *Too much coffee this morning.*

In the stall, she undid the bib to her overalls and pulled them down around her knees. In the cold air, her urine stream was warm, a welcomed relief from her full bladder. She heard two women talking at the sink about the outbreak.

"We'll be lucky to keep our jobs. I heard GEO may go bankrupt," one woman said.

"I definitely won't be supporting a union now. We'll be lucky if any of us get to keep our jobs," the other woman said.

Stella buttoned up her overalls and flushed the toilet. When she heard the women leave, she stepped out to wash her hands. She looked in the mirror and took a deep breath before heading over to the HR trailer to see what Maria wanted.

Across the parking lot, on the second floor of the main office building, Roger sat at the head of the long table in GEO's executive conference room. The incident management team, consisting of department heads and senior managers from marketing, sales, operations, and finance, sat around the table. It was the fourth straight day of meetings with investigators, and his team was not happy to be working around the clock.

"All hands on deck. Our focus today is on staffing and scaling down. We've already seen our sales numbers go down."

"There will need to be immediate cuts," Roger's COO Brendan Conley said.

"Easy for you to say," an operations manager said. "They're not in *your* department."

Roger raised his hand to interject.

"We'll review every department. Obviously ops is going to see the most immediate and drastic cuts, but we'll also be reviewing sales and marketing. A small core team of us will be dealing with the media, the Feds, the lawyers, and the insurance agents. I need the rest of you to focus on running the business. At the end of the day, we are still the nation's largest organic salad company, and I intend to keep it that way. Jane will keep you informed on the outbreak as needed. If you have any questions, my door is always open."

The group stood to leave and filed out of the room. Roger turned to Jane and motioned for her to come closer.

"Can I see you in my office?"

"Of course."

CHAPTER 23

Outside in the parking lot Emiliano was holding his own meeting. He too was in full damage-control mode. The few dozen authorization cards he had collected were unsigned, a worrisome sign that he didn't have the support he needed.

"I know you're nervous and don't want to think about organizing," he told a small group of coworkers in the lunch trailer. "But this is when we need a union the most. The FDA ordered the disposal of more than two thousand cases of finished product this morning. We're being redirected to dispose of thousands of plastic clamshells we packed this week. The cases are piled twenty feet in the air behind the shipping docks awaiting transport to the nearest landfill. Now, doesn't that make you a little nervous about your future? A union would prevent them from firing us."

The small group looked uncomfortable. A young, new employee challenged Emiliano.

"We are lucky to have jobs. Why would we want to jeopardize them by forming a union? My landlord said his mortgage payments went up last month, so he doubled my rent. I need this job!"

"Emiliano is right. This is the exact time we need a union," another said. "To protect our jobs."

"We can't let a twenty-four-hour cable news cycle ruin our momentum," Emiliano said. "This will blow over, and everything will be back to normal in a week."

"Then I say we wait until that happens before stirring the pot," the new employee said. Emiliano saw his supervisor walking toward the trailer.

"Enough for now. I will keep you all posted."

The group dispersed at the sight of the supervisor and headed back toward the growing pile of discarded clamshells.

Stella sat down in the waiting area of the HR trailer. She listened as curious coworkers asked about the outbreak and the company's new health-care plan. People were upset about the company's new high deductible plan implementing a $5,000 increase to their out-of-pocket expenses. The open cubicles made it easy to hear everyone's questions and HR staff's scripted answers.

"Does the company pay for immunizations?" one woman asked the HR generalist behind the desk. "Under our old plan, my children got all their shots."

"Our new plan is designed to give you more control over how you spend your health-care dollars. We're suggesting that you take your children to the free clinic for shots. They are covered by the county."

"But we have to wait for hours there, and they're closed by the time our shift is over."

"You can schedule an appointment on your day off or wait until our employee health fair in the fall."

The girl at the reception desk turned toward Stella.

"Stella, Maria is ready to see you now."

Stella stood up, nodded, and smiled. As she walked into the office, she sensed an uneasiness with Maria Hernandez, an HR manager who had worked her way up the ladder. She sat down in one of two chairs opposite Maria's desk. Framed pictures of children laughing and swinging their feet over the bow of a sailboat were neatly arranged for visitors to admire.

Maria was a second-generation Mexican American. Her parents had worked in the fields when GEO was just starting. Maria grew up stocking shelves and ringing up items at the Roadside Stand. The Worthingtons appreciated her parents' work ethic and credited her father with some of their early farming successes. They rewarded loyalty and had realized the value of promoting someone like Maria. She was their token Latina success story, the single employee they pointed to whenever anyone asked if it was possible for Mexicans to rise in the ranks at GEO. It was as if Kate thought promoting Maria benefitted every Mexican worker.

Maria's primary job was to oversee GEO's biannual move to the desert. It was a colossal task to hold company-wide orientations in both California and Arizona and keep track of more than one thousand employees who were fired every November and rehired each spring. It was like closing and starting a new business every six months. Essentially GEO employed two separate workforces—one in Las Flores and one in Yuma, Arizona. Maria was a bilingual master at managing both.

Like Stella, Maria had worked there for fifteen years. She was a bridge, someone who could communicate with the production line workers and report back to senior management. She wore a gray suit and heels, just like the women in sales and marketing. Stella tried not to shift in her chair, self-conscious of the noise her ski overalls made. Maria started to speak before Stella could compliment the pictures of her children.

"Thanks for coming in this morning, Stella."

Stella took off her bump cap and placed it in her lap.

"Kate and Jane are planning the annual employee meeting and wondering if you'd be willing to speak about our quality control procedures, you know, from the wash-line workers' point of view? You are on the front lines every day."

"Me?" Stella asked.

"Yep, you. Kate wanted someone who has worked here a long time and seen the changes as we've grown."

"What does she want me to say?"

"Oh, not too much. Maybe just a five-minute talk on how you sort and prep product for testing and shipping. You'll be up onstage with Kate. We're trying to give all the employees a better idea of how each department participates in Green Earth's mission every day."

"You mean like how we sort out wilted romaine leaves and look for foreign objects?"

"Exactly."

"Sure, I guess I could do that. I wouldn't want to say no to Kate."

"Excellent. I'll let her know, and we'll be in touch with some talking points for you."

Stella stood to leave, but Maria continued.

"There's one other thing. We've decided to rearrange some employees for cross-training, and I noticed you've been subbing for Blanca Rivera on the night shift. Would you be okay taking that shift as your regular shift?"

"Blanca needed help. It was just one night."

"Well, we're working on a new rotation that focuses on cross-training, and we think it would be a good way for you to increase your skills."

"I'd rather not be transferred permanently. My daughter, Esperanza, and my mother are home nights, and I have to take care of them. I thought the B shift was assigned to new workers? I've been here for fifteen years."

"We understand these shift changes are sometimes hard to manage with your other obligations, but we think it's important to rotate so employees can learn new tasks and fill in where needed. You will be assigned to our new Clean and Clear program, in charge of pulling samples to be tested for pathogens. We can't risk another widespread contamination, and we need to emphasize our food safety priorities. This will look good in your file."

Maria smiled and tried to put a positive spin on the news.

"Do I have a choice?"

"You always have a choice, Stella," Maria said flatly. "You don't *have* to work at Green Earth Organics."

"I understand. When do I start?"

"B shift employees clock in at four p.m. We'll see you here at four p.m. sharp Monday then, when training begins. You can take the rest of today off."

Just be glad you have a job. It's better than having to go to the community kitchen. God will get me through this. He always does. Esperanza doesn't need me as much as she used to, she's busy with volleyball and senior year. I can do this. It's temporary.

Ofelia walked toward her in the smock room, gesturing for Stella to come closer.

"What did she say?"

"Emiliano told me they couldn't retaliate, but Maria just put me on the B shift. It has to be because they know about the union vote."

"Did she say anything about the outbreak? What about the union?"

"Not a word. But I could tell she knew. You can just feel it when they're not telling you something. She said something about 'cross-training' and rotation, but I know it's because they found out about the union. They're trying to intimidate me."

"That snake. There's only two months left in the season. They'll put you back on A shift when we start up again, won't they? After this E. coli investigation passes, no?"

"Who knows. She also asked me to speak at the employee meeting next month, something about representing the operations department. I think it's their way of keeping an eye on me. Emiliano is right. They don't appreciate what we've put into this company. I may as well have started yesterday."

CHAPTER 24

Sedona, Arizona

After her massage, Kate went to Dr. Hukura's office, where she was asked to wait in a small reception area. Sheer, magenta-colored gauze curtains hung around the walls fluttering in the breeze. Lavender and gardenias lined the walkway, a burst of color amid the orange and beige desert. Water cascaded down a small pile of rocks on a low table in front of Kate's deep leather chair, calming her. As she waited for her name to be called, she closed her eyes and practiced her deep breathing exercises.

"Kate?"

Aurora, a tall woman, extended her weathered hands toward Kate. Her wrinkled skin was sun-damaged and makeup free. She had long, gray hair that she wore pulled back in a neat, low ponytail with a silver-and-turquoise Native American clip. She wore a flowing dress with a tie-dyed pattern.

"Please, come in."

Aurora motioned toward her office and gently led Kate into a small sanctuary lined with orchids and simple charcoal sketches of waterfalls.

"Welcome. Have a seat."

Kate was apprehensive. She couldn't stop thinking about what was happening back home. She recalled a friend who had told her that Aurora worked miracles and had saved their marriage.

I can handle my own marriage, thank you, but my professional life could use a little direction.

Aurora sat opposite her and calmly folded her hands into her lap. She crossed her legs and looked at Kate directly.

"So, you are here to learn about your future?"

"Yes, that's right."

Kate was beginning to relax, grateful to be away from the chaos back in California.

"I see." Aurora leaned forward and held her hands out to Kate. "Let me hold your hands."

Kate reached across a small ottoman between their two chairs and put her hands in Aurora's. They were soft and smelled like jasmine. Aurora closed her eyes and rubbed her fingers along Kate's thumbs.

"I see big things ahead for you, Kate. You will be hugely successful, and you and your husband are going to be very wealthy. Your company is in the midst of a challenge right now—a public relations challenge that will either break or propel you."

Kate looked straight at Aurora.

"Can you be more specific? What kind of challenge are you talking about?"

She must have seen the news about the E. coli outbreak. Aurora ignored the question.

"There is a disconnect. Your heart and your mind are not in the same space."

Kate leaned forward, hungry for more.

"A disconnect? What do you mean?"

Aurora let go of Kate's hands and held her palms over Kate's shoulders.

"I see Mother Earth trapped. People are suffocating for lack of air. Birds and fish are dying. It has something to do with your business model. Have you moved away from your original passion? Something has changed that is causing uncertainty and disharmony."

Kate nodded, wide-eyed.

"How can I realign my heart and my mind?"

It must be the outbreak. She knows about the outbreak. My worst fears are coming true. I will be defined by E. coli. The GEO brand will be forever tainted.

"What is it? What disharmony?"

"Plastics. I see piles and piles of plastics littering waterways and filling landfills. Chemicals from the plastic are leaching into streams and oceans causing an imbalance in our natural systems and our bodies."

"Plastics?"

Kate looked white. She was incredulous and began to sweat with panic. "No, no, you don't understand. It's *sustainable* plastic! They make it out of recycled water bottles, and we're actually reusing it! We use the *good* kind of plastics. We have *scientists* working on this. What do you know about the packaging industry anyway? I came here to find out about my future, not get some lecture on ocean pollution. What kind of a doctor are you anyway? Are you a real MD?"

Flustered, Kate stood to leave.

"I'm a naturopathic doctor. Kate, I just relay what I see. It's not always what my clients want to hear, but I hope it helps guide you and your decisions. Thank you for your time."

"You're wrong about this. We are organic. We're helping clean up pollution, not make it worse. We remove pesticides from the soil and we plant trees!"

Goddamn Roger. He promised that the plastic packaging was not a problem. I knew it would come back to haunt us.

Back in her room, Kate called Jane.

"This is Jane Janhusen. I can't take your call right now, but please leave a message, and I'll get back right to you. Thanks!"

Fucking voice mail. Why won't she pick up?

"Jane, it's me. I just met with your friend Aurora. Packaging is the devil of the industrial food system, and we've got to do something about it. It's even worse than E. coli. Plastic clamshells are the only things holding me back from being recognized as the nation's premier authority on organics and environmentalism. We have to address the waste issue by coming up with something better, something that isn't dependent on foreign oil, chemicals, massive energy inputs, and landfill space. Something we can be celebrated for, just like baby greens. Call me back as soon as you can." She turned off her BlackBerry and threw it on the bed.

GEO's core customer base, the same people who flocked to the company for its organic salads and small farmer story, were the same ones who detested the clear plastic packaging. Kate had heard of new technologies that were making bags more breathable. Plastics with tiny holes that let the greens stay fluffy and dry and took up a fraction of the petroleum and landfill space than clamshells. Maybe GEO should be investing in that rather than the millions of clear shoe boxes they produced? Or maybe it was just time to get out.

Kate returned to her room feeling less relaxed than when she arrived. She regretted meeting with Aurora so early in her visit. Her mind raced with images of the plastic bags littering a beach surrounded by dead fish scattered like trash.

How could I not have seen this coming? Of course the plastic packaging would be a problem. It weighs more than what's inside.

It was the one thing critics pointed to when they talked about GEO. That and the fact that they didn't pay higher wages. But packaging is what really bothered Kate. She could justify the low wages by saying they were creating jobs, even turning applicants away every season. But there was no excuse for filling landfills with garbage or killing wildlife. Shipping salads across the country was another environmental stress. She rationalized the predicament, going over and over it until she felt a headache coming on.

At GEO, we want everyone to have access to fresh fruits and vegetables. No one else can grow them like GEO can. Plastic clamshells fulfill our mission to distribute organic vegetables to the masses, and until someone comes up with something better, that's what GEO will use.

Critics had it so easy, always coming up with what companies were doing wrong, but never offering a solution. She would show them. She would go home and direct Roger to invest in state-of-the-art packaging facilities that others would imitate. GEO would move beyond salads and become the benchmark for environmentally friendly packaging.

Kate could feel her anxiety turn to a determined excitement about innovation. Aurora was right: there were big things ahead for GEO. They would go beyond produce to become the nation's "leading organic *food* company."

Despite her momentary panic attack, the Euclid was proving to be just what Kate had needed: a week for her to get away and look at things with a new perspective. She would turn the packaging issue into a win before they sold GEO. Aurora's words stuck in her mind. *Uncertainty and disharmony.*

She took notes in her Moleskine folio. She would set up a sustainability committee to look into how GEO could innovate their packaging. She made a list of priorities and would meet with Jane to go over them her first day back.

CHAPTER 25

Cedar Rapids, Iowa

Bucky was still moving in and out of consciousness. He was agitated and hallucinating. His tiny body was limp. He was hooked up to a metal IV stand that hovered over his bed with eight bags that delivered fluids directly into his veins.

Ruth and Scott sat by his side. When the doctors entered, they both stood to greet them.

"How are the IVs working?" Dr. Ryan said. "Do we need to adjust?"

"We call it the octopus," Scott said.

"He looks calmer this morning. Has he been able to sleep?" Dr. Ryan asked.

"On and off," Ruth said. "He told me he saw bugs crawling all over his bed."

"That's a common side effect. The CT scan came back normal though, so that's a good sign. It tells us there's been no brain damage. We need to make sure he stays hydrated."

Ruth and Scott awaited every test result with apprehension and took each morsel of positive news as a sign God would get them through this. Ruth was learning a whole new language of medical terms and medications.

"I'm concerned Bucky's mental state may be due to metabolic acidosis," Dr. Ryan said.

"What does that mean?" Ruth asked.

"It's a relative increase in total body acid, another side effect of the kidneys not properly processing blood. His symptoms are numerous, but we can mitigate each one. Your job is to stay positive for Bucky and know that he is receiving the best care possible. Our team is monitoring every move, and I want you to be comfortable to ask any questions you have. I've consulted a top nephrologist, and he has recommended we insert a Tenckhoff catheter for peritoneal dialysis."

"Can you say that in English?" Scott said. "What does a nephrologist do? He never even took Tylenol before three days ago. And what is a *tank off?*"

"*Tenck-hoff.* Nephrologists are doctors who specialize in kidney diseases. Dialysis prevents the kidneys from shutting down. Bucky's aren't working properly, so we have to do the work for them. Dialysis will clean his blood and get it back in his system so he can fight this. Tenckhoff is a type of catheter, a little tube we insert to help drain the fluid from his abdomen. It will require a surgery and be uncomfortable to put it in, but once we have it in place, he should be more stable."

"Surgery? I just don't know how much more his little body can do on its own. Why couldn't this have been me?" Ruth said.

"Ruth, even if this had been you, your body would be able to fight it off easier. The elderly and children are much more susceptible to E. coli O157. Your immune system is established, and you are a strong, physically fit person. These outbreaks affect the most vulnerable first. Kids don't have the same defense mechanisms as adults, which puts them at a higher risk."

"I know. I just wish I hadn't given him that smoothie."

Scott put his arm around her shoulder.

"This is no one's fault, sweetie. You can't waste energy blaming yourself. We need to focus on getting him home. He'll be playing ball in the backyard again before you know it, you'll see."

Ruth gave him a half smile and hugged him back. She could feel his cell phone vibrating. Scott looked down at the screen and handed her the phone. "It's your mom."

"Hi, Mom. How are the kids? Do they miss me? Are they behaving?" She put it on speakerphone for Scott to hear.

"Of course. We all miss you and Bucky. We're saying our prayers together every night, and the boys are being really good. Brianna's been taking the bottle, and she slept for six hours straight last night. It's like they're all rallying for their big brother."

"I miss them so much. I just want to come home with Bucky and get our lives back. I promise I'll never complain about all the stupid things that used to bother me again—clothes on the floor, an overgrown lawn, piles of laundry. It all seems so trivial now."

Scott rubbed her back. "Ruthie, please don't blame yourself for this. You didn't know that spinach was contaminated. None of us blame you. You know that, right?"

She nodded, tears welling up in her eyes. She motioned to Scott to stay and walked out in the hall to talk to her mother out of Bucky's earshot.

"I saw on the news that there's another little girl in Ohio. And that woman in Wisconsin who died. Have you heard anything more about whether it was E. coli?" Ruth whispered.

"We haven't been watching the television. I'm going to feed the children now, but I'll check in later. Don't worry about us, Ruth. We're all fine."

Ruth returned to the room and scanned the local newspaper for information about other victims.

Bucky was waking up from a nap and tried to sit up when he saw Scott.

"I brought you a little something, Buck." Scott said.

"Daddy!" he said quietly, his voice raspy from all the medications.

His arm was strapped down and connected to the IV fluid bag. Scott pulled up a chair and took a book and stuffed dog out of the bag. Ruth smiled as she watched Bucky's mood lift at the sight of his father. He idolized Scott.

"Thomas the Train! Thank you, Daddy. Can you read it to me?"

"You betcha, buddy. I got this little doggie too. Maybe when you get better, we'll go to the pound and pick out a real puppy."

"Really?"

"Really. I promise."

Ruth smiled and nodded in agreement when Bucky looked to her for confirmation. A puppy would mean Bucky had made it through. It would be a constant reminder of how lucky they were to have him back home. Scott smiled and lifted his hand to give Bucky a high-five.

"I'm getting better, Daddy. Stronger every day. I miss Brady and Brian and Brianna."

"I know, Bucky, I know. We'll be back home soon, and you can play in the backyard with them again. They can't wait to see you, Buddy."

CHAPTER 26

Stella walked in the house and greeted Gran and Esperanza, sitting at their usual spots at kitchen table. She dropped her lunch bag and took off her bump cap before sitting down.

"What are you doing home so early?" Esperanza asked.

"Do you want the good news or the bad news first?"

"Did you get fired?" Gran said. "I knew that Emiliano boy was trouble!"

"You haven't answered my question."

"The bad news," Esperanza said.

"They moved me to the B shift."

"I knew it! They're watching you, *mija*. All that talk of unionizing. You need to stop that! What's the good news?"

"They didn't fire me. And I can drive Esperanza to school in the morning now. But you two are on your own from four p.m. to midnight."

Stella rubbed the back of her neck. She was sore from a long day of chopping lettuce.

"You're going to need sleep in the mornings. You can't stay up for twenty-four hours," Gran said.

"Don't worry, Mama. I can take care of Gran," Esperanza said. "We'll be fine. I just wish they would recognize all you've done for them. Did they give you a raise too?"

"No raise," Stella said. "But they did tell me this will look good in my file. Something about being cross-trained and flexible. Maria also asked me to speak at the employee meeting next month. Maybe I'll announce onstage that we're forming a union."

"You've really lost your mind, *mija*. No one is going to vote for a union in the middle of a recall. They're all happy to have jobs."

"I don't even want this job anymore. I'm working on a way to get more of the dollars floating around in the world to come our way. Like sardines into a whale's mouth at feeding time. Why should GEO be the only whale in the ocean, taking all the sardines? I work just as hard, even harder. I'm going to start my own home farming business and be my own boss."

She patted Esperanza, who was checking her phone and not paying any attention. "Is Raul coming over again tonight? You two are spending lots of time together."

"*Sí*, mama. He's been helping me with my algebra, and that's why I'm getting an A."

"Well, just make sure you two stick to algebra, okay?" Stella smiled.

"Mama! What else would we be doing?"

"I don't know. You tell me. Gran tells me you two go in your room and close the door. You know I don't like that."

"We're just listening to music. We're not doing anything, I promise."

She glared at Gran who pretended not to hear the conversation and continued working the flour to make her tortillas.

"I trust you, *mija*. You just have to use your good judgment and make good choices, okay? Especially if I'm not going to be around as much. As long as your grades are high, I guess I can't complain much, can I?"

"That's right! I met with my college counselor today, and she said I have all the classes I need to apply to Berkeley. Don't worry about your job. I'm going to get a good job and take care of you and Gran. You'll be able to quit GEO, and we'll move into our own house."

"What about Raul? Where does he want to go?" Stella was happy to change the subject from GEO to Esperanza. Focusing on Esperanza always put things into perspective.

"He wants to go to Berkeley too. He can get in. His grades are better than mine, and he plays three varsity sports. He's still working on getting his citizenship though so he can't get any financial aid. He's a DREAM Act kid – came to the U.S. with his parents when he was a baby. His mom didn't even tell him he wasn't a citizen until last year. We're still thinking of going to visit the campus next month. He may not be able to go to college next year, but he will someday. Mrs. Murphy said there's a bus trip to three colleges."

"You'll be so far away," Gran said.

"No, I won't! It's only three hours north, Gran. I can come home whenever I want."

Gran muttered, "But you won't."

Stella smiled and stood to start dinner, patting Esperanza on the shoulder.

"Raul is not the only dreamer. We're all dreamers. I dream of you not having to work the night shift. That will be worth going away to college for."

CHAPTER 27

Saturday, September 6, 2008

Saturdays were normally quiet at the Las Flores facility, staffed only by a skeletal sales team to take orders. This weekend was different. Roger called in managers to be available for federal and state investigators. They combed fields around the plant and took soil and water samples.

"They are determined to pinpoint the source of the contamination, and we have a fucking bull's-eye target on our back," Roger said.

"Maybe being the largest shouldn't be the goal. The little guys don't have these problems. Local farms are thriving, and all they talk about is being fresh and familiar. Large isn't always good to consumers," Jane said.

"Small farms aren't worth six hundred million, either," Roger said.

Jane handed him the press release issued overnight by the CDC.

"Here's what they've said to the media. At least it's a weekend; maybe this story will run its course by Monday's news cycle," she said.

> **Centers for Disease Control and Prevention, Atlanta**
> *FOR IMMEDIATE RELEASE*
> *September 6, 2008*
>
> *As of 1 PM (ET) September 6, 2008, 80 persons infected with the outbreak strain of E. coli O157:H7 have been reported to CDC from 15 states.*

The elderly and children are particularly at risk. E. coli O157 was isolated from 13 packages of spinach supplied by patients living in 10 states. Eleven of the packages had lot codes consistent with a single manufacturing facility, Green Earth Organics in Las Flores, Calif., on a particular day. Two packages did not have lot codes available but had the same brand name as the other packages. The "DNA fingerprints" of all 13 of these E. coli match that of the outbreak strain.

Advice to Consumers

The following is advice for consumers about this outbreak:

- *Consumers should not eat, retailers should not sell, and restaurants should not serve spinach implicated in the E. coli O157:H7 outbreak. Products implicated in the outbreak include fresh spinach and spinach-containing products from brands processed by Green Earth Organics.*
- *If consumers cannot tell if a brand of fresh spinach was implicated in the outbreak and the package has a "use-by date" of August 29, 2008 or earlier, they should not eat it.*
- *E. coli O157:H7 in spinach can be killed by cooking at 160° Fahrenheit for 15 seconds. (Water boils at 212° Fahrenheit.) If spinach is cooked in a frying pan, and all parts do not reach 160° Fahrenheit, all bacteria may not be killed. If consumers choose to cook the spinach, they should not allow the raw spinach to contaminate other foods and food contact surfaces, and they should wash hands, utensils, and surfaces with hot, soapy water before and after handling the spinach.*

Roger flung the paper back on the table.

"We're the only company they named?"

"We knew that was coming," Jane said. "It was that or be accused of not cooperating."

After their fieldwork, the investigators planned to meet with all of GEO's department heads and review production processes from start to finish. Roger knew they would pick over every aspect of the business with a fine-tooth comb. He was determined to prove this could have happened to any company.

"E. coli is an act of nature that just happened to land on some spinach leaves in one of our fields. Our friends in the Salinas Valley are getting off unscathed," he said.

Jane followed him across the hall into the executive conference room where a small group was standing around the television with sullen faces.

"What's the latest?" she asked.

"A woman in Wisconsin died last night. They think it was E. coli. James Bogey is popping champagne as we speak," Gregg Fluerant said.

"Who is James Bogey?" one of the managers asked.

"Bogey, Appell & Huffington—the country's top personal injury law firm, always looking for the next food-borne illness or consumer product defect."

Jane rocked back and forth with her arms crossed.

"If people are dying, it's considered a public health issue," she said.

"That's why we will say we are fully cooperating. Public health is our number one concern," Roger said.

He gave the television a dismissive wave.

"Turn that off," he said. "We've got work to do."

He took the seat at the head of the table. Jane sat down in the chair to his right, notebook in hand.

Roger sat up straight and cleared his throat, a signal for the room to quiet down.

"The next several months will test the company's strength like nothing else. But we will show that Green Earth Organics cares about public safety and will do everything in its power to prevent another outbreak from happening again. We'll turn this into something positive. We'll work with the country's top food safety scientists to develop new testing methods for E. coli, and we'll take full responsibility for our processes. We'll take care of every victim and prove that Green Earth Organics cares about health. We are, after all, a company founded on *enriching the earth*. Now I need people to get back to work and focus on your teams. We can't have everybody distracted by this. We do still have a company to run. We can't allow this to bring us down. Jane and I will be handling all media and will call upon each of you as needed for expertise when we need to respond to something. No one is to speak to a reporter directly. We have to run every response through attorneys, understood?"

The group nodded in unison.

"In the meantime, I want everyone to focus on their department and to make sure your targets are being met. We'll need to refocus sales to make up for the past week. Are there any questions?"

The group was silent.

"Good. My door is open if you think of any."

They shuffled out of the conference room.

Jane's most important task was to preserve Kate's reputation, even before responding to attorneys or federal regulators' requests for information. When she got back to her office, the message light on her phone blinked red like a silent siren. Calls from reporters, colleagues in the organic industry, and food safety interest groups filled her machine. She quickly assigned the reporter calls to Caroline.

"Call each one back and tell them we are cooperating with the FDA completely to find the source of this contamination," she said. "Don't say anything else. If they push, tell them we'll be issuing a statement soon."

Roger's name flashed across her phone screen.

"That's all for now. Thank you, Caroline. Please close the door."

She hit the speaker, and Roger's voice filled her office.

"We need to shred all documentation that shows we rushed orders. I want every e-mail, every phone message, and any paperwork that refers to a rush in July and August destroyed immediately." She picked up the receiver in case Caroline was listening through the door.

"Is that legal?"

"If we don't ask counsel, then we don't know, do we?"

"I guess not."

"So we don't know."

"Well, don't you think we should consult the attorneys first? I'm pretty sure that would not be looked upon favorably."

"Look, Jane, this is not a matter for you to worry about. Trust me."

"But we keep daily operation logs too, Roger. We were clearly pushing the facility to its limit in the past few weeks. We moved record amounts of product and were trying to process it all to make sales targets. And there were several sick employees the day the contaminated product was packed."

"Why do they come to work sick?"

"We don't offer sick pay. They can't afford to lose those hours, Roger. It's an ongoing issue Maria has warned you about."

"What issue *doesn't* Maria warn me about? Can't they just be happy to have jobs? Listen, this could have happened to any company. We follow the highest safety protocols in the industry. It was a freak accident that E. coli landed in a couple of our bags and then decided to reproduce like rabbits. Fresh produce is a game of Russian roulette every day, and this time the bullet hit us."

Jane wasn't about to argue with him over strategy. *It's just a bump in the road for our public relations. A minor detour, even if our products are killing grandmothers and toddlers across the country.*

"I need a break from lawyers and scientists," Roger said. "I'm supposed to meet with some VC guys in town tonight. They're on their way to LA. Are you free for dinner?"

Jane checked her watch.

"I don't know. What time?"

"Seven. Paloma Grill."

"Sure, I can do that."

"Good. I'll see you there."

CHAPTER 28

Dr. Ryan emerged from the operating room smiling and gave Ruth and Scott a thumbs-up.

"You've got a tough little fighter in there. The catheter is in, and he should be back in his own room in the next two hours," he said.

"Any news on when we can bring him home?" Scott asked.

"I'd like to move him to the pediatric intensive care unit for monitoring, but if all goes well, I don't see why we can't send him home in the next few days. We'll repeat peritoneal dialysis four to six times a day and ease him off that as his vital signs improve. We're looking out for signs of anemia and a decline in his BUN and creatinine. But I think we've turned a corner. Stay strong, Mom and Dad."

Dr. Ryan's youthful energy made the Malmquists feel at ease. They knew the staff at St. Luke's was giving Bucky the best care possible, and for the first time in a week, they began to feel confident they would get through this.

"We can't thank you enough, Dr. Ryan. I can't even imagine losing him," Ruth said.

"Well, we're lucky he's such a strong little guy. We've also confirmed that Bucky's stool samples match the O157:H7 strain associated with the outbreak. It matches the same strain the lab found in the spinach bag you turned in."

"That will make it easier to trace, right?"

"Federal investigators are working on that. I am not in the position of giving you legal advice, but there are attorneys who can help you," Dr. Ryan said.

Scott and Ruth had briefly discussed liability, but were so focused on Bucky's health they had not contacted an attorney. There were dozens of unanswered messages on their home phone from attorneys, insurance companies, media outlets, and friends checking in. But Ruth had been adamant that they not focus on anything but Bucky.

"I need all my energy to get him better and back in our own house, but thank you, Dr. Ryan."

"Totally understand. Let's see if we can make that happen then," he said.

Dr. Ryan cleared Bucky for visitors, and for the next two days, the Malmquists had a steady flow of friends and relatives visiting his hospital room. His numbers were improving, and when Brian and Brady came to visit, he showed the first signs of getting back to normal. He was eating again, and the nephrologist said they could remove his catheter. Brian was so excited to see his older brother he climbed up the side of Bucky's bed and crawled in next to him for a hug.

Scott convinced Ruth she should get some rest and sent her home to be with Brianna. When she walked in the door, Ruth took Brianna from her mother's arms and savored the sweet smell of her baby skin.

"Mmmmmm! How's my tasty baby?" She kissed her on the cheek.

Her mother had already bathed her and fixed a homemade dinner.

"Let me get the boys ready for bed while you nurse the baby," her mother said.

"Thanks, Mom," Ruth said. "It feels so good to be home. I hate that Bucky isn't with me though."

When she opened the door to the boys' bedroom she could see they were already sound asleep. They were sprawled on top of their covers like snow angels in the carefree way toddlers sleep. Brian's little pajamas were inched up so she could see his belly button. She gently moved the covers over them and kissed each one softly on their foreheads as she said a quiet prayer to God that Bucky would be home soon.

When she returned to the dining room, her mother had a warm plate of chocolate chip cookies and a glass of milk ready for her.

"Yum. This is so much better than the hospital cafeteria," she said. "Thank you for everything, Mom."

Ruth sat down and devoured the cookies with Brianna in her lap.

"Everyone at church is praying for you. They've organized enough meals to feed Scott and the children for a year."

"Let's hope we won't need that."

"There are some messages on the phone for you. A bunch of attorneys asking about a class action lawsuit and some reporters."

Ruth was too tired to process all the information.

"I'll listen to them tomorrow. Tonight I just want to go to sleep in my own bed and pray that Bucky will be home soon."

She awoke at 2 a.m. to the sounds of Brian moaning in pain. She walked down the hallway to check on him and immediately smelled a diaper change coming.

"What is it, sweetie? I'm right here."

He was limp, and she could feel his high temperature as soon as she picked him up and carried him into the bathroom to the changing table. Ruth grabbed a baby wipe as she undid his soiled diaper and saw blood in Brian's stool.

CHAPTER 29

Jane arrived early at the Santa Lucinda Golf and Country Club and settled in to an overstuffed chair in the lobby adjacent to the Paloma Grill. The grill was popular watering hole and sat on the edge of a bluff overlooking the Pacific Ocean. It was easy to see why Roger loved the place so much. She admired the massive redwood beams that spanned the twenty-foot ceiling. *Rustic meets preppy.* She tried not to stare at the couple snuggled up with glasses of wine. They were whispering into each other's ears by the stone fireplace that emitted crackling sounds and the spicy smoke of an oak-burning fire.

The GEO entourage arrived right on time. Roger led the pack across the lobby toward where she was sitting. Tony followed with a young new sales rep on his arm. Gregg Fluerant walked behind Tony talking with two private equity partners.

"You made it," Roger said. He greeted Jane with a wide smile.

"Wouldn't miss it," she said.

Roger turned to the two men with Gregg.

"Mike, Frank, this is Jane Janhusen. She runs our communications and marketing department."

"Nice to meet you," Jane said.

She held out her hand to each of them.

"Likewise. Mike Millies with Summit Capital."

"My pleasure. Frank Camillo."

The group proceeded into the dining room and sat at a large, round table in the corner. It was good to get away from Las Flores for a few hours. The incident management team had been working around the clock for the past five days with lawyers, scientists, insurance agents, and regulators on the outbreak investigation. Roger took the seat next to Jane and skimmed over the leather-bound wine list.

"Red or white?"

"Mmmmm. Probably red. The grilled grass-fed rib-eye sounds amazing."

Jane turned her attention to Gregg.

"How is Kathy?"

"She's great. Getting ready for the first grandchild," Gregg said.

"Oh, that's wonderful. Congratulations!"

The waiter approached the table with a stack of menus.

"Do you have any questions about the wine list, Mr. Worthington?"

Roger went immediately to the cabernet sauvignons, his favorite red varietal.

"How is the 2003 Heitz Cellar Cabernet?"

"Excellent choice. Known for its aromas of fresh-picked blackberry and cassis. It balances a classic Cabernet richness with silky tannins on the palate, charming and complex."

"Perfect, we'll have that."

He snapped the menu shut and folded his hands in front of him.

"So, gentlemen, tell us why Summit is a worthy partner for Green Earth Organics."

Mike and Frank looked to each other to answer.

"I was thinking you should tell us why we should consider buying Green Earth," Mike said. "We've done our due diligence, but I think there's been a few developments in the past week that could affect those numbers. Wouldn't you agree?"

"We'll see. Our insurance coverage is solid. And Jane here has done a fine job fielding all the calls. We're cooperating fully and want to put the whole thing behind us as soon as possible," Roger said. "We're going to turn this outbreak into a win for GEO. I'm already using it to learn about improving traceability from farm to table. We want to champion transparency. It shows integrity and builds customer trust. It also allows companies to identify and troubleshoot real-time supply chain issues, strengthening both our business and reputation. It's absolutely the right thing to do."

Mike and Frank nodded. Jane had to give him credit. He nailed the talking points.

The waiter returned to the table with the wine wrapped a white napkin around the neck and held it out to show Roger the label. He nodded approval before he poured. Roger sniffed, swirled, and tipped his glass up to taste.

"That's nice." He nodded. "Very smooth."

The waiter filled the other glasses halfway, the first of several rounds that would follow. By the end of the main course, the group had polished off three bottles, and by 10:00 p.m., Roger was in no shape to drive home. He directed Gregg to handle the 7:00 a.m. conference call with the investigators so he could sleep in. With Kate gone, he had asked his assistant to book a room earlier in the day.

The group shook hands and agreed to meet again once the media frenzy died down.

"I'll have my assistant follow up to schedule a tour of your facility," Mark said.

"I look forward to it," Roger said.

Jane stood next to him and smiled politely.

"Nice to meet you," she said.

Roger turned his back toward them and smiled at Jane. Tony and his date were cuddled up at the bar ordering after-dinner drinks. She was pulling his tie toward her and leaning in for a kiss.

"Best to leave those two to themselves," Roger said. "Hey, we're looking to expand into a new line of personal care products, and I was hoping to ask your opinion on a few things." He smiled, gesturing for her to sit down. Roger didn't have the social graces to hold a door for a woman, but he did know that buying her a drink usually relaxed her.

"I'll have a Crown Royal. What can I get you?"

Jane had heard of Roger's flirtations with women in sales but had never witnessed them firsthand. She felt suddenly guilty for not calling

Kate back yet. It had been such a crazy week, she had barely had time to feed her cat.

"Oh, I'll just have a glass of water," Jane said. "I have a long drive home."

"So, I've been working on a plan to source organic herbs and fruit to put into a line of oils and lotions. Do you think there's a market for that?"

"Sure. Women are always looking for new beauty products. I think an organic line would sell, especially if we can find local sources for the ingredients and market them as supporting family farms."

"I was thinking of looking to Chile and China actually. It's much cheaper to source from China, and it is *the* emerging market of the world. I'd like to start learning more about it."

"Well, that's true, but you can't be sure of the organic integrity. And wouldn't it take a lot of time and energy to ship from there? China may be a leading market for manufacturing circuit boards and cell phone memory chips, but I'm not so sure about perishable commodities, especially organic. They get low marks on organic integrity, and they're known for allowing harmful materials into their production lines, things like lead and other poisonous metals. I don't think that's something Kate would want to be associated with, Roger."

"We could monitor the production. And as far as transport costs, I would have the whole line produced close to the source. It's cheaper all around to pay third-world workers than to open a new facility here in California. This is the worst place in the world to do business. The regulatory constraints and taxes are going to run off anyone who wants to make a profit."

A waitress brought over his Crown Royale and placed it on a cocktail napkin.

"Just water for you, Miss?"

"Yes. Thank you," Jane said. She watched Roger write his room number on the tab and wondered how long it would take him to invite her up for a drink.

"It's so noisy in here. Would you like to go back to my room where it's quiet, and we can sit out on the patio? Look out at the ocean. Have you seen the views from this place?"

That didn't take long.

"I should probably get going. I have a long drive."

"C'mon. Just one nightcap. It's on me."

"All right, but just one, and then I really need to get going."

The landscaped grounds surrounding the clubhouse were impeccably kept, with manicured lawns and meandering pathways for golf carts and walkers. She followed him along the dimly lit pathway from the bar to his room and watched as he fumbled for his key, buzzed but not quite drunk.

"Can you hold this?" he asked, handing her his drink while he looked in his pocket for the key card. "Where did I put the key card?"

She stood quietly, gauging the situation and regretting following him back to the room.

"Maybe I should just go, Roger. It's getting late, and we have another full day of meetings tomorrow."

"No, no. Here, I have it right here," he said triumphantly and swiped the card to quickly open the door. "I enjoy being with you, Jane. Just stay for one glass of wine."

Jane looked around, noting her exit possibilities.

"So, you were saying that you think sourcing from Chile or China would be more profitable?" she said.

"Yes. That's really the direction all manufacturing is going, you know. Sit down and relax for a minute. Would you like me to take your coat?"

"No, I really can't stay long, Roger."

"You don't have to drive home. You could stay here."

He pulled a DVD out of his leather duffel bag.

"Do you ever watch porn?"

"Not with my boss."

"Well, let's pretend I'm not your boss tonight. It's muuuch easier when you compartmentalize the different aspects of your life, Jane. I got a movie with a brunette in it. Juz like you." He leaned in toward her face as Jane stepped back.

His phone rang just as she was about to chastise him for putting her in a difficult position.

"Hi, sweetie," he said, and then mouthed the word *Kate* and rolled his eyes.

"Yes, everything is fine here. How is the Euclid?" He paused. "Don't worry, all the work will be here when you get back. Umm-hmmm. Love you too."

He flipped his phone shut and moved toward Jane, placing his hands on her waist.

"Sorry about that. She is so needy. But she's in a whole other state tonight… and not going to be back for a few days."

Jane was light-headed from her third glass of wine. She stepped backward and sat on the edge of the bed. He stood over her and ran his fingers through her hair. His cologne smelled fresh even though they were four and half hours into the night.

"You are soooo beautiful. I think about you all the time."

He began to caress her shoulders. She tried to stand up, but he pushed her backward and she fell onto the bed.

"This is so much more fun than being on a conference call with those assholes at the FDA," he said, nuzzling up to her ear and kissing her neck. "When you watch me being interviewed on the national news, now you'll know what I have tucked away under my pants…"

So he was one of those. Dirty talk. So cliché. And repulsive coming from a drunk boss.

He fumbled with his belt buckle. Her barriers were down. She didn't want to offend him. Before he could go any further, a loud knock on the door interrupted them.

"Room service!"

Jane straightened her skirt and sat up.

"I'll get that," she said. *There is a God. I love room service.*

She wriggled out from underneath him and stood up.

"I really should get going, Roger. Thanks for a fun night."

She grabbed her coat and purse and slid out the door as the bellman rolled a cart past her with a bucket of champagne and two glasses.

CHAPTER 30

Ruth knew she had to get Brian to the hospital as soon as possible. She called her mother to come back over and watch the children and then called Scott to let him know she was on her way back to the hospital.

"He's only two, Scott! Dr. Ryan said toddlers are most at risk…" She was babbling now, in a panic as she packed a bag for Brian. "How could this happen? It's been a week since he drank the smoothie. Do you think it was the kiss he gave Bucky at the hospital? Dr. Ryan cleared Bucky for visitors."

"Ruthie, calm down. We have the best care possible. Look at how well they've taken care of Bucky."

"I'll be there as soon as I can. My mother is on her way."

Ruth hung up the phone and went back to check on Brian. He was barely responding to her and wouldn't eat or drink anything. She rubbed his back and tried to feed Brianna, too distracted to nurse, praying that God would save her sons. Reluctant to turn on the television or pick up the stack of newspapers that had piled up on the kitchen table, she told herself it was important to stay informed on how the investigation was going. She wanted to see if there were any more reports of illnesses. She picked up the latest edition of the *Cedar Rapid Gazette*.

Green Earth Organics Recalls Thirty-One Thousand Cases of
Packaged Spinach
Contaminated Spinach to Blame for Hundreds of Illnesses in
Nationwide E. coli Outbreak

Green Earth Organics announced it is voluntarily recalling over thirty-one thousand cases of Herbal De-Lite and baby spinach due to spoilage concerns. In a statement, the company said it was made aware that "a possible E. coli contamination" has been linked to its products.

"Public safety is our first concern. We are working with federal and local officials and fully cooperating with efforts to find the source of the contamination," the company stated on its website.

The affected items were produced in August 2008 and distributed nationally. The recalled products have specific Julian codes between LF220A and LF235A and a "best by" date of August 29. A complete list of affected products can also be found on Green Earth Organics website. The company notes that the recall is being initiated "out of an abundance of caution" and that it is working with the FDA to remove the products from store shelves. Consumers who have purchased these items are urged to throw them away and contact Green Earth Organics (with proof of purchase) for information on reimbursement at 1-800-243-1690.

Brianna looked at up at her, wide-eyed. Ruth's tears streamed down her cheeks and dropped onto the tiny hand clutching the side of her breast. She wondered if Brianna could sense the panic that had overcome their little family.

"Grammy is on her way, sweetie. She'll stay with you and Brady, okay? Mama has to go back to the hospital for a couple of days to see Bucky and take care of Brian." Brianna stared at her, still kicking her feet.

When Ruth's mother arrived, she helped her gather her bags and latch Brian into his car seat.

"It'll be okay, Ruthie. Everything will be alright," she said.

"I'll call you when I get there," Ruth said. She strapped Brian's limp body into his car seat and waved to her mother standing in the driveway with the baby.

When they arrived at St. Luke's emergency room, Scott came downstairs from Bucky's room to meet her at the admitting desk. A team of nurses and doctors were waiting for them. They admitted him immediately while the nurse on duty asked Ruth the same questions they had with Bucky: "What has he eaten? When did you notice symptoms? How long has he been lethargic?"

Ruth, disheveled and tired, answered patiently with Scott by her side. He was holding her hand, silently trying to assure her everything would be okay.

"This is different, Scott. He's not as old as Bucky, and his symptoms seem much worse to me. How could this happen? I thought we were out of the woods. He kissed Bucky yesterday. Do you think he's still contagious?"

The nurse showed no reaction but took notes as Ruth spoke.

"Why don't you go upstairs and sit with Bucky. I'll stay here with Brian," Scott said.

"This is such a nightmare. I can't even believe we're going through this again."

Ruth took the elevator up to the PICU and walked down the dark corridor to Bucky's room. It was still predawn, and the floor was quiet and dimly lit. A skeletal staff of night duty nurses sat at the central station.

"Hi, Ruth! It's good to see you. Bucky is doing so much better. I think Dr. Ryan is going to release him tomorrow," one of the nurses said.

Ruth tried to smile but felt like crying. She wanted more than anything to hear that news and celebrate, but she would never be whole again if she took only one child home.

CHAPTER 31

Monday, September 8, 2008

On the first day on her new shift, Stella was called into a meeting with her supervisor to be briefed on the Clean and Clear program's new protocols. Every salad would be tested for pathogens before it went out the door. A shiny new bump cap was sitting on the desk when she arrived for the meeting.

"You'll be given a new cap color, now that you're assigned to quality control. White is the QC color code," her manager said.

"But I was a manager on the A shift. Am I no longer a manager?" She wanted her red hat back, the one that took her ten years to earn.

"Not until you finish your QC training. In QC, we like to stress the importance of teamwork. We are only as strong as our weakest link. Every person's job is as important as the next," he said.

He handed Stella a new hat with GEO's green and brown logo and "S. Gonzalez" printed out above the forehead.

QC training took four hours. New employees were put in a conference room and required to watch a video about the new safety system. Every outgoing packed case would be tested for E. coli and held for shipping until it was verified to be clear of any pathogens. Stella's new job entailed pulling a random bag out of each case and removing a handful of leaves for testing. Each bunch would need to be removed, placed into a test bag, labeled, and placed on a cart that another person took to the lab.

Once they watched the video, employees were asked to fill out a short questionnaire to see if they understood the process and sent on their way to begin the shift.

I can do this. It's just a few more weeks. Then I will start my own home farming business and leave GEO behind forever.

She missed her friends from the A shift. Emiliano had suspended the union vote until after the outbreak investigation was complete. He said there was no use holding a vote he knew they would lose. And Ofelia's lunch break counseling sessions would have to take place over the kitchen table from now on. The only good thing about working the B shift was that she didn't have to stand for as many hours. The QC team rotated in and out of the samples lab, and she got to sit in the lab for hours, carefully printing out labels identifying each sample to be tested for pathogens. By the end of her shift at 1 a.m. her feet were not nearly as tired as they used to be.

CHAPTER 32

Brian's bed in the ICU at St. Luke's was surrounded by tubes pumping fluids into his system. Dr. Ryan had assigned a hospital psychologist to the Malmquists and advised Ruth and Scott to meet with her the morning after Brian was admitted. The three of them sat in her small office near the ICU.

"Bucky is only five, and we don't want his healing to be affected by another stressor," she advised. "He might even feel guilty that he's getting better while his brother is not."

Scott shot her a dirty look.

"Brian will get better," he said.

"Of course, I didn't mean to imply—"

"You're a psychologist. How could you not know how your comments affect us?" Scott said. Ruth sat next to him, staring ahead.

Ruth stood up and walked down the corridor to get some fresh air. Everything was happening so quickly; she didn't know what to expect next. In just one week her world had been shattered. She didn't want to hear any more from doctors. She wanted to go home with her sons and have their life back. In the past seven days, she had been home for just a few hours, weaned her daughter prematurely, and watched two sons fight for their lives.

When would this nightmare end?

Scott caught up with her and told her Dr. Ryan was looking for them and that they needed to come down to the ICU immediately.

Brian lay on the bed, hooked up to tubes with an oxygen mask covering his mouth. Dr. Ryan met Ruth and Scott at the doorway.

"Ruth. Scott. I'm so sorry. I have to warn you: Brian is not responding to treatment as well as Bucky did. He is younger, and his organs are simply not as strong to fend this off."

"What about a catheter? Can't you put a catheter in? Give him an IV, antibiotics, anything. Whatever you did for Bucky that worked." Ruth was frantic. "You must be able to do something! You have to save him!"

Scott had his arm around her shoulders and was listening to Dr. Ryan. "I'm so sorry, Ruth, but there is nothing more we can do. His kidneys are shutting down faster than we can pump fluid into his system. The CAT scan shows he has already had significant oxygen loss to the brain."

"What does that mean? What does it mean? Is he going to die?" she said.

"His heart, lungs, and kidneys are being kept alive by a machine. His organs just don't have the strength to do what they need to do. At this point, the best we can do is manage his pain."

"*Manage his pain?* That means he's dying. Oh my God, Scott."

She turned toward her husband and buried her face in his broad shoulder. Ruth was shaking uncontrollably. Scott wrapped his arms around her and drew her close. He looked up to the ceiling and prayed that God would take his son peacefully. He turned to Dr. Ryan.

"Can we have a moment please?"

"Of course. I'll be right here if you need me."

Ruth and Scott stood over Brian and laid their hands on him to pray.

"Dear God, please take our boy and watch over him," Scott said quietly. "Welcome him into paradise and bless his soul."

Ruth sobbed quietly as Scott leaned down to kiss Brian on the forehead.

After several minutes, Scott called Dr. Ryan back into the room and told him they were ready to disconnect all the tubes attached to Brian's limp body. When they removed the mask, Brian's lungs couldn't pump on their own any longer and the exhausted organs slowed to a stop within minutes. Ruth climbed into the bed to cradle her son wishing she could transfer her heartbeat to his. She smoothed his blond locks and whispered into his ear. "Don't be afraid, sweetie. The angels will take care of you."

This is God's will. No more unbearable abdominal pain, vomiting, or diarrhea.

Two nurses spoke in hushed tones in the hallway.

"Cardiac arrest after multiple seizures. It came on so fast."

Convulsions. Gasping. Ruth told herself he hadn't felt any of it, that he was already gone by that point. It was just the physical reaction of a body losing its life. His soul had already flown. She and Scott stayed in the room with Brian until Dr. Ryan pronounced him dead and lifted the sheet over his head.

Ruth was too numb to be angry. Her confusion and complete shock at the past six days had left her so exhausted she could barely breath.

There is a reason for this. One day God will help me understand. God loves him. God will save him. He is with Jesus now.

In the hallway, they watched as a hospital crew put on gloves and removed Brian's tiny body from the bed and placed him on a gurney to be transported. Scott and Ruth prayed over him. A bishop from their church had arrived to pray with them as they removed the body. Ruth wept quietly while Scott stood stoic and silent by her side.

CHAPTER 33

Las Flores, California
Tuesday, September 9, 2008

After the B shift, the early morning air was cool on Stella's face. Clouds blocked the moonlight. She fumbled for her keys under the dim parking lot lights and turned on her car heater as soon as the engine started. The drive home took less time at 1 a.m. There were hardly any other cars on the road.

She noticed an unfamiliar white truck parked on the street as she turned in to her driveway and parked in her usual spot next to the three stairs that led to her front door. She turned off the engine and gathered her bump cap and lunch box from the passenger seat before opening the car door to go inside. Gran forgot to leave the porch light on.

I'm going to have to remind her to leave on the light.

She closed the car door and turned to walk toward the house when a figure appeared out of the shadows and blocked her path.

"Sorry, I didn't mean to scare you. I was in the neighborhood and thought I'd stop by to see how the new shift is working out." She could smell liquor on his breath and recognized Jimmy Migliozzi's nose right away.

"Jimmy. You startled me," she said as she reached in her pocket.

"I know. It's a little late. But I was on my way home and just decided to make a quick pit stop."

"Kind of late to be out and about, isn't it?" she said.

"I was driving by on my way home from Philly's Bar. Ever been there?"

"Not in a few years, no."

"Oh, you should go. They make a mean margarita."

Stella stood her ground, trying to appear calm. Her heart was racing.

He stepped closer to her, his breath warm on her face, and put a hand on her shoulder.

"You should not be here, Jimmy."

At six feet one inch, he was almost a full foot taller than her. She stepped to his right, but he mirrored her move to block her path. She moved again, this time to the left. He stepped left to block again. She turned to run back toward her car when he grabbed her from behind and put his hand over her mouth. She could feel his lips on her ear.

"Don't try to scream or get away. This will only take a minute."

Stella elbowed him in the stomach and tried to wriggle out from his grasp, but he was too strong. In an instant, she could feel his hand groping her before he shoved her face-first into the side of the house and ripped off her jacket. He grabbed the strap on her overalls and pulled it loose. The metal clasp flew through the air. She felt the cold air on her skin as he pushed her shoulder against the house and held her still with his left hand while he unzipped his pants with the right. He fumbled to get his pants down. Stella wriggled as he tightened his hold on her. Her fingers and jaw clenched as she felt him thrust violently into her from behind. She closed her eyes and counted until he was finished. After he came, he pushed off her, pulled up his pants, and fastened his belt. He reeked of cologne, whiskey, and cigarette smoke. She slumped to the ground, leaned over, and heaved vomit onto the ground.

"I'll pad your punch card to compensate for the extra time tonight," he mumbled. "And let's keep this between you and me. I wouldn't want you to lose your job or anything. You've already managed to be demoted once this month."

Crouched on the ground, she pulled her legs close and put her forehead on her knees as she listened to his boots crunch the gravel in her driveway. Her cat screeched as he kicked it on the way to his truck.

Stella didn't move until she heard the engine start and drive away. Before getting up, she reached into her pocket and pulled out her phone. The light from the kitchen window cast a dim glow. She looked down to make sure she could see what she was doing as she clicked off the Record button.

PART III

Farmers

CHAPTER 34

Jane had spent all of Monday in the fields with investigators taking soil and water samples. She welcomed the excuse to not see Roger. On Tuesday morning she was walking Emily and Jerry through a typical sanitation routine when Kate called from The Euclid.

"Jane, it's me. We need to talk. Why haven't you returned my call?"

She excused herself to take the call.

"Hi Kate, I'm sorry I haven't called. I've hardly had time to take a pee since Wednesday."

Kate's nervous energy jumped out of the cell phone. She pelleted Jane with questions, leaving no space to respond.

"How is everything going? Are the investigators still there? I heard a woman died in Wisconsin—is that true? Are they sure it was from spinach? From *our* salad? How about the *Forbes* interview? How did Roger do? I'll be back on Saturday."

"I'm meeting with the FDA right now. Can I call you back?"

"I met with Aurora. I know I promised I'd stay away, but I just need a quick update. And I have to tell you what Aurora said! She says we have to do something about all our plastic packaging and focus on alternatives and new products if we are to survive."

She knew better than to cut Kate off.

"We had to cancel the *Forbes* interview. Insurance company attorneys don't want Roger talking to any press until this blows over. There are too many pending lawsuits," Jane replied calmly.

She looked up to see Roger approaching. They hadn't seen each other since his little stunt at the Paloma Grill Saturday night. He walked right past her into the meeting without acknowledging her.

What an ass. So glad I left when I did. Thank you, room service.

Kate kept talking, telling Jane about the Euclid's amazing food and the yoga classes. She sounded much better than the rest of GEO's management team. Maybe it was turning out to be a real retreat after all. It was just what she needed and timed perfectly to coincide with a self-imposed media blackout.

"What? *Forbes* didn't happen? I know you have to go, but call me back as soon as possible."

"I will, Kate, with a full update."

Jane hit the disconnect on her BlackBerry and walked down the hall to the bathroom. She looked in the mirror, wiped her smudged eyeliner, and reapplied her lip gloss. Had it been just a week since the FDA called? It seemed like an eternity. She could barely remember what her job was pre-outbreak. *What did I used to do all day?* Her life had become an endless stream of meetings with investigators, phone calls seeking permission from attorneys for every statement GEO issued, and navigating the landmines of every new illness report that could lead to death. *Our mission is to advance the production of organic agriculture to enrich the earth. Mother Nature is such a shitty business partner.*

When she returned to the conference room, investigators were questioning Roger about the sick employees on the day the contaminated spinach was packed.

"So far, all the collected bags shared a common link: they were all produced during the same shift on the same day at the same plant in Las Flores," Emily said.

Roger sat in his usual chair at the head of the table.

"GEO's policy is not to have workers come in sick, so we may have been a few people short in early August when several workers called in sick," he said.

"Does that mean you were short-staffed so some of your processes could have failed?" the lead investigator asked. "Or that the workers that were there were sick?"

"No, we have procedures in place to accommodate absent employees," Roger said. "Our wash logs show every step was followed."

"There are some logs missing from the days in question," another investigator said.

"I can't speak to that. You'd have to check with our quality control officer."

"If you can't speak to it, we'll be including in our report that protocols were not followed. Missing production logs are a violation of OSHA rules and your own standard operating procedures."

The group stood to leave when Jane's phone rang again.

Caroline Boyd

Jane had decided to use the employee meeting as an opportunity to promote GEO's new Clean and Clear program and celebrate the company's renewed commitment to food safety.

"I think we can turn this meeting into a win-win," Caroline said.

"Why don't you look into organizations working to raise awareness on food safety? I'd like to invite a speaker to talk at the employee meeting. Maybe even someone affected by the outbreak so we can show people we're tackling this head-on. I want to drive home that Green Earth Organics is committed to providing safe and healthy food. We're going to lead the industry in new testing protocols for fresh produce," Jane said.

"I'll have Stella Gonzalez come by your office this afternoon to go over her presentation," Caroline said.

"Sounds good. Finally, something is going right," Jane said.

CHAPTER 35

Stella awoke with a throbbing headache and sore back. She heard Gran and Esperanza in the kitchen clanking breakfast dishes and talking about a volleyball game that afternoon. She got out of bed and walked over to the mirror to examine her face. It was 7 a.m. She fumbled for her phone out of her overalls pocket and hit the speed dial button for Ofelia. No answer.

"Offie. Call me as soon as you get this. I need to talk."

Jimmy had shoved her so hard against the house that her left cheek had a scratch on it from the stucco siding. When she turned to examine her back in the mirror, she saw a purple and yellow bruise forming where he had pushed her rib cage.

"*Ese pedazo de mierda*," she whispered to herself.

His threats left her shaken and scared. Instead of calling the police after the attack, she had undressed and showered. She wanted to get Jimmy off of her. The warm water soothed her and washed her tears down the drain. She wouldn't call the police, not yet. She didn't know what to do, afraid that no one would believe her. It would be Jimmy's word against hers. *How can I jeopardize my job, our house? Everything I've worked for to provide a stable and happy life for Esperanza and Gran?* She was as much ashamed as she was angry. *I should have screamed. I should have never tried to talk to him.*

Shaking, she knelt down at her bed to say a Hail Mary and ask God for guidance. After a minute of silent prayer, she put her phone next to her painted armadillo and placed her wet underwear in a sealed Ziploc bag in her nightstand drawer, nestled between a Bible and a rosary.

Jimmy had left all the evidence she would need.

Gran stood at the stove stirring eggs as Stella entered the kitchen.

"What happened to your face? Is this what they do to you on the B shift?" Gran said.

"It's nothing. I scraped it on a carton I was lifting, that's all."

No need to traumatize all of us. I need to protect them.

"Good luck with your game today, *mija*," Stella said.

"Thanks, Mama. Coach says I'm starting!"

Stella was distracted. She knew she had to report Jimmy's attack, but she had heard stories about the local police not believing rape stories and even accusing Latina women of being at fault. Her mind replayed the events over and over again in her head. Guilty thoughts formed a loop of questions.

What did I do wrong? How could have I prevented it? I should have screamed as soon as I saw him. How could I be so stupid? Did I do something at work to encourage it?

After Esperanza caught her bus, Stella went back to her room to get dressed and left a second voicemail for Ofelia, who was still working the A shift. Gran was cleaning the breakfast dishes in the kitchen when Stella re-appeared in the kitchen.

"Do you want to come to mass with me this morning?" Gran said.

"I was going to ask you the same thing," Stella said.

Later that day, she clocked in at GEO right on time for the B shift, 4 p.m. sharp. Jimmy would be gone for the day, hopefully. She was still trying to figure out what to do. *Who will believe me?*

Her new supervisor handed her a note as she was changing into her smock.

"Stella, please stop by my office before your shift. I'd like to discuss the employee meeting and your presentation. Thanks, Jane Janhusen."

She folded the note and put in her pocket before walking across the yard to Jane's office in the main office building. Jane was distracted, shuffling papers on her desk when Stella appeared in her doorway.

"Hi, Jane," Stella said.

Jane spoke without looking up.

"Stella! Come in. Thanks for agreeing to speak at our meeting. We've had such a crazy week with the outbreak investigation. I am happy to be focusing on something else for a few minutes."

Stella tried to cover the bruise on her cheek by holding her hand over it. Jane didn't seem to notice and kept shuffling papers as she spoke.

"I know public speaking can be intimidating, but we'll have a PowerPoint for you to follow, and you're good at talking about your work anyway. I've watched you talk to your team on the floor, and you seem at ease."

Stella stood up straight.

"There's something I'd like to talk about before we get to the employee meeting."

"Sure. How is the B shift going?"

"Jimmy Migliozzi came to my house this morning drunk. He's my former supervisor from the A shift."

"What did he want?"

"What do you think he wanted?"

"I don't know. I've heard stories he can sometimes act inappropriately with some of the women on the lines."

"Well, the stories are true."

Jane looked up.

"What do you mean?"

"He attacked me in front of my house and then threatened me. He said I could lose my job if I told anyone."

"What do you mean by 'attacked'?" Jane looked confused.

"He shoved me against the side of my house, ripped off my overalls, and raped me. Then he pulled up his pants, told me not to tell anyone, and kicked my cat before driving away."

Jane put down the stack of files in her hand and looked directly at Stella.

"Stella. I don't even know what to say. These are serious accusations."

"I am telling the truth."

Jane turned white. She fidgeted in her chair and tapped a pen on her desk.

"We'll have to file a report. Why didn't you call the police?"

"I didn't know what to do. I don't trust the police, and I was scared. I didn't want to wake my mother or Esperanza. And he told me I would lose my job if I said anything. I tried talking to my priest, but he left too soon after mass this morning. I don't know who else to talk to."

Stella started shaking. She was too agitated to cry, but Jane could see she was upset and genuinely scared of what Jimmy could do. Jane walked around her desk and sat next to Stella, not sure what to say. She put her hand on her knee to soothe her shaking.

"Don't worry. You won't lose your job or your house. He's not above the law. I need to talk to Roger about what to do next, Stella. I'm so sorry. Are you hurt? Do you need anything, to see a doctor or take the day off?"

"I need to see Jimmy Migliozzi held accountable."

"Of course. We have policies in place to take care of this sort of thing, even if he is a supervisor."

Stella nodded and took the packet Jane had prepared for the employee meeting.

"I will practice my lines and be ready to present at the meeting next month," Stella said.

"Thank you, Stella. And let me know if you have any questions on the presentation."

CHAPTER 36

Jane went straight to Roger's office as soon as Stella left.

This should be interesting: reporting a sexual assault to someone guilty of sexual harassment. Let's see how well you compartmentalize this, Roger.

She breezed past his assistant into his office, closing the door behind her. He was leaning back in his chair with his feet propped up on the desk, talking to Sheila Connors on the speakerphone. They were discussing GEO's strategy for the onslaught of lawsuits coming their way. Sheila's voice boomed out of the speakerphone.

"It doesn't matter. Even if you could win in court claiming this was an act of nature, you will always lose in the court of public opinion. Do your growers have secondary insurance we can tap into? Because we're going to need it," Sheila said.

"I'll have Gregg look into that. I'm thinking a reserve of one hundred million dollars in claims here," Roger said.

Jane stood in front of his desk with her arms folded, waiting for him to finish the call. He motioned for her to take a seat.

"Leafy greens is all the rage for these personal injury attorneys jumping on this gravy train. You can thank me for tripling your billable hours."

"I'm not complaining. I have another call to take. Call me as soon as you get Bogey's first demand letter," Sheila said.

He hung up and clasped his hands behind his head, smirking at Jane.

"Back for more? I knew you would change your mind."

"Speaking of sexual harassment, I have something to discuss with you."

"Who said anything about sexual harassment? I thought you were having a good time." He smirked at her.

"I'm not talking about Saturday."

"What is it then? Did my brother get caught getting a blow job from another sales rep?"

"Roger, this isn't funny. I just had a wash-line employee stand in my office and tell me Jimmy Migliozzi showed up at her house this morning drunk and attacked her!"

"What do you mean *attacked*?"

"I mean *attacked*! Rape. We have a supervisor who *raped* an employee this morning."

Roger took his loafers off his desk and sat straight up in his chair.

"How do you know this employee isn't looking to make a little money? Does she have any proof? Did it happen on-site?"

"I believe her," Jane said, disgusted. "She has a scratch on the side of her face. She's telling the truth."

"Has she told anyone else?"

"You are asking all the wrong questions, Roger. We have to report this to the police. We don't need another out-of-control incident on our hands. I'm advising you to take this seriously. Even if you don't get what the problem is."

"Don't lump me in with rapists, Jane." His tone was serious. "I know I can get a little frisky after a glass or two of wine, but I'm not violent. A late-night booty call is not the same as rape."

"Whatever, Roger. GEO does not need its supervisors being accused of rape on top of everything else we are dealing with right now."

"I'll deal with this. Who is she anyway?"

"Stella Gonzalez. She's been with us for fifteen years. Lives over on the east side, and apparently Jimmy showed up at her house early this morning after her shift was over. She's supposed to speak at the employee meeting next month."

"Jesus Christ. Why didn't she call the police?"

"I don't know. She said she was scared and didn't know what to do. Jimmy also told her not to tell anyone or he would see to it that she lost her job. She's a single mom and takes care of her mother."

Jane watched him for some sign of outrage. She could see that Roger was upset, but maintaining the calm crisis mode he had been for the past week, a real master at compartmentalizing his professional and personal lives. Roger always took care of his own. Jane wondered how well he would take care of someone else though. Someone who couldn't give him anything back or praise him with adulation at holiday dinners and social gatherings. Wasn't that the sign of a truly good person? Giving when you didn't expect anything in return?

"I'd like to meet with her. As soon as possible."

'With Stella?"

"Yes. I want to her version of the story before I drag Jimmy's ass in here."

CHAPTER 37

Wednesday, September 10, 2008

When Stella arrived for work the following day, Jane was waiting for her in the smock room.

"Roger would like to meet with us," Jane said.

Stella had never been upstairs in the main office building before. Roger greeted them in his doorway.

"Stella. Hello, it's good to see you. Please, have a seat," he said.

Stella sat without saying a word.

"Jane, would you mind closing the door?"

Jane shut the door behind them and sat down next to Stella.

Roger sat forward and folded his hands on the desk in front of him. He looked directly at Stella.

"Let's get right to the point. Jane told me what happened at your house Tuesday morning."

Stella nodded, avoiding eye contact with him.

"First of all, I want to apologize for any misunderstanding you may have had with Jimmy. I know sometimes he can be a little rough around the edges."

Stella sat quietly, listening. She looked at Jane for a reaction, confused. *Had Jane told Roger a different version of her story?*

"Misunderstanding? Roger, I told you what happened. This is not *a misunderstanding*," Jane said.

He held up his hand signaling Jane to be quiet.

"Let me finish. I'm prepared to compensate you, Stella, if we can just keep this incident quiet. As you know, we are in the middle of a national E. coli outbreak, and we really don't need any more distractions for our employees or management."

Stella looked to Jane for direction.

"Roger, this is not something we can sweep under the rug. Jimmy is a liability and poses a threat to Stella and other women—"

"Jane, please. I will handle him. Right now we are talking about Stella. You will not lose your job or your home, Stella. You have my word. In addition, I'd like to offer you some compensation that will enable you to purchase your home outright. You could own it and not have to worry about ever being evicted or paying rent again."

"I can't condone this, Roger. This is not what we discussed," Jane said.

"This is an offer for Stella, not you."

Stella didn't know what to say. She knew Jimmy needed to be reported, but how could she tell Roger Worthington no?

"Are you asking me not to report this to the police?" Stella asked.

"That's exactly what I'm asking, Stella. I will purchase your home, put the title in your name, and write you a check for ten thousand dollars to help pay for your daughter's college education, your mother's care, and anything else you want. There are no strings attached."

"No strings except my silence," Stella said.

Jane looked at Stella and shook her head.

"Stella, if you need time to think about this, that's fine. We do not expect you to make a decision right here," Jane said.

"Yes, that's fine. But I do ask that you keep this between us. If anyone else finds out I will have to rescind my offer."

"I understand," Stella said, barely audible and looking at the floor.

"And just so this doesn't drag on, I'd like an answer by tomorrow. I will talk to Jimmy in the meantime, and I can assure you he will not bother you again."

"I understand."

"That will be all. Thank you, Stella."

Jane stood to leave and turned to give Roger a cold glare as she followed Stella out.

As they walked back toward Jane's office, neither of them said a word until they got to her door.

"I'll understand if you don't want to speak at the employee meeting, Stella."

"Can I think about it?" Stella said. "I have to get back to my shift."

"Of course," Jane said. "Take all the time you need."

Stella returned to her job pulling samples from cases ready to ship. She labeled each bag with the date, lot code, and production run.

I'm not going to let Pinocchio determine my fate. I will speak at the employee meeting, and I will show Roger that I am not intimidated. I've worked hard for this company, and I will leave on my own terms.

Later that night during her break, Stella stepped outside and called Ofelia again.

"Where have you been? I've been trying to get ahold of you since Tuesday!"

"It's ten p.m. Stella! I can't help it if Pretty Boy got you assigned to the B shift! I'm in bed by the time you get home!" Ofelia said.

"I need to talk to you. Pinocchio showed up at my house Tuesday morning drunk."

"I knew it! He was always staring at you funny. What did he want?"

"What do you think? He shoved me up against the house and raped me."

"Oh my God, Stella! Are you okay? What did he do? Have you reported it?"

"I'm bruised. And he scratched my face. I didn't know what to do. I can't tell my mother or Esperanza. I told Jane and she reported it to Roger. They want me to take hush money."

"What? How much? Have you told Emiliano?"

"Ten thousand dollars. And he said he'd pay for my house. But it doesn't matter how much. I'm not going to take it."

"What did Pretty Boy say?"

"I haven't told him yet."

"Why not? Maybe he can get the union bosses to get you more!"

"Offie, I don't want their money. It's dirty money. I'm going to the police."

"What if they don't believe you?"

"I have evidence. Keep this between us for now, Offie. I need to talk to Emiliano and then figure out what to do next."

"Of course. I won't even tell Bobby. Can I pick you up tonight?"

"No, go to bed. I'm going to ask Emiliano to meet me after work. I'll let you know if he can't. Thank you, Offie."

Stella hung up her phone and dialed Emiliano's number.

"This is Emiliano. I can't take your call right now. Please leave a message, and I'll call you back if I like you."

"Emi, it's me, Stella. Can you meet me at my house after my shift tonight? I need to talk. Thanks."

She snapped her phone shut and returned to her station, rubbing the bruise on her back but feeling stronger than ever.

CHAPTER 38

Thursday, September 11, 2008

Emiliano was waiting when Stella pulled into her driveway. She felt a wave of relief at the sight of his car.

"You're here," she said. They embraced in her driveway.

"Of course I'm here. What's up? They can't put you on a worse shift."

"It's Pinocchio. He was here Tuesday morning when I got home."

"What was he doing here?"

"You can imagine what he did."

She looked directly in his eyes.

"I'll kill him. Did he hurt you? Are you okay? Have you called the police?"

"I reported it to Jane and we met with Roger yesterday. He wants me to take ten thousand dollars not to talk."

"Bastards. They won't get away with this."

"I want to go to the police. This morning."

"I'll take you there right now."

Stella hugged him and started to cry.

"I can't take that money. It would condone what he did. I wouldn't even be able to spend it without feeling ashamed. I will not let what he did determine my future or Esperanza's. We don't need Roger's money for her college. She will go to Berkeley on her own merits."

"Of course she will," Emiliano said. "You are stronger than they know."

When they got to the police station, a female detective led them into a private room for an interview. Stella answered her questions, describing every detail of the attack.

"I think you should get a DNA sample from the suspect and see if it matches the one I have here," she told the detective as she handed her the Ziploc bag with her underpants in it.

The detective examined the bag and put it in a bin to be analyzed by the crime lab.

"This is helpful for your case, Ms. Gonzalez, but I have to warn you: he can still claim it was consensual. This shows no proof of force. There are no witnesses, and we don't have a rape kit to admit as evidence."

"You should also take this," Stella said.

She handed him her cell phone and asked that they make a copy of the recording from 1:16 a.m. on Tuesday morning.

"You can also take a picture of the bruises on my face and back," she said.

The detective took the phone and led Stella into a separate room to photograph her. By the time they finished it was 6 a.m.

"We reviewed the recording. It's a little muffled, but clear enough to hear his voice and a struggle. Nice work. That will be all. We'll keep you informed and let you know as soon as we have him in custody."

"Thank you," Stella said.

Emiliano turned to her and put his arm around her shoulder before leading her back to the car and taking her home. They drove in silence, watching the sun rise over the fields surrounding Las Flores. The oak trees curved with the shape of the hill, windblown for centuries, yet strong and unwavering. An orange glow filled the morning sky as they pulled into Stella's driveway. She could smell the garlic and onions Gran was sautéing on the stovetop. She turned to Emiliano and gave him a hug.

"Thank you, Emi. Will you join us for breakfast?"

"As long as your mother let's me in."

CHAPTER 39

Tipton, Iowa

The Malmquists arrived at the LDS church dressed in their church clothes. It felt like every person in Cedar County was there. Hundreds of people poured out of the church. Family and friends from as far away as Pennsylvania and Idaho joined the locals to line up and greet Ruth and Scott. They stood at the front of the church politely thanking people for coming and hugging each person. Ruth was buffered by people who loved her. In Brian's two years on earth he had made his mark.

She was exhausted. She had not slept a full night since Bucky got sick and was still numb at the thought of burying a child. Brian's four-foot pinewood coffin was lovingly cut and sanded by Scott's brothers, woodworkers by trade. It was a simple box, a reflection of the family's deeply held religious belief that salvation was not found in material things. Simple rope handles and a flat lid made it look more like a large crate than a casket.

Ruth stood silent over her son's body. He had been dressed in a white suit and laid inside the baby-blue satin-lined box. He looked so peaceful, with his little hands folded over his chest. His face was pale and relaxed, as if he was just sleeping.

He is at peace now. This is the intersection of my life: a bubble, floating between "before" and "after." Nothing will ever be the same once I walk out of this church, that box sealed forever. I will never be in the same room with him again. What is the word for a mother who loses a child? Not widow. Not orphan. There is no word to describe me now. How do I stop time? Rewind the clock? I feel like Jackie Kennedy, defying her elegant pink suit, crawling over the trunk of an open convertible chasing a piece of her husband's skull, desperate to reassemble him into the whole he was a split-second earlier. It's no use. He is already gone. Where is he? I hope he is safe. Breathe. Focus on this moment. I can still touch my son. I will kiss him one more time before the box is sealed, before his body is taken away from me forever.

Scott touched her arm.

"Ruthie, it's time to begin."

She focused and took her seat at the front of the church. Their family felt so small. Bucky was still at home with Ruth's mother, under Dr. Ryan's orders to rest. Brady sat on Scott's lap, well-behaved and quiet, while Ruth cradled Brianna in her arms. Their large extended family surrounded them. Ruth appreciated being part of a community that stuck together.

After the service, friends and family gathered in the church hall, sharing stories and pictures of Brian. A slideshow of his baby pictures played on a loop above tables filled with Crock-pots and funeral potato dishes. Pictures of him laughing and playing with his brothers and Scott in their backyard made Ruth smile. He was always trying to keep up with Bucky.

Brian's death would be a catalyst for her. His short life inspired them to take action and seek out others who had suffered from the outbreak. He would not be forgotten. Within hours after his death, Scott had set up a memorial website to honor Brian. "Brian's Project" would be their way of educating others about foodborne illnesses and how to avoid them.

When an attorney called shortly after the service to inquire about suing, the Malmquists politely declined. They would have no part profiting from the tragedy of Brian's death.

"This was God's will. Please respect our privacy," Scott said. He hung up before the attorney could go on.

CHAPTER 40

Las Flores, California
Friday, September 12, 2008

The Feds were moving faster than anyone anticipated. Environmental scientists and epidemiologists had been working around the clock for ten days comparing soil samples, spinach collected from victims' refrigerators, and stool tests from county health departments.

"I feel like we're the lead role in a CSI episode," Roger said.

The FDA had scheduled a 10 a.m. conference call on Friday to announce a major development in the case. Jane had called the incident management team to listen in together. The group was reviewing staffing levels and finalizing new protocols for the Clean and Clear program while they listened to bad music on the line and waited for the FDA to start the call.

A voice interrupted the music at 10:10 a.m.

"This is Mark Manusco from the CDHS." Jane's stomach was turning. She hadn't eaten breakfast and was already on edge about Stella's situation.

The week from hell is almost over.

"Good morning. Thanks to everyone on this call. I know you've all put in a considerable amount of hours these past few days, and I want to let you know how much we appreciate that. We're announcing this afternoon that we have isolated the same E. coli strain found in the product samples and matched it to water and soil samples from fields leased by Green Earth Organics in Las Flores, California," he said.

Jane took notes as everyone stared at the speakerphone, silent.

They're so excited they're wetting their pants.

Mark continued.

"We found that the E. coli O157:H7 infections had matching PFGE patterns among two hundred and eight people in twenty-four states. This is the genetic marker we've been looking for. In the past ten days, this investigation provided laboratory and epidemiologic evidence implicating bagged spinach that was traced to a single processing run at Green Earth Organics in Las Flores, California packed on August 19. With this finding, we have decided to conclude our on-site field investigations. We will continue to monitor PulseNet data for reports of illness, but we believe the numbers have peaked and will start to decline. We are also advising the public that it's safe to eat spinach."

Roger cleared his throat.

"This is Roger Worthington with Green Earth. Can you tell us how the E.coli got onto the spinach?"

"Could have been anything. Water, wildlife, a bird overhead. Our field investigation showed a broken fence where we think wild pigs may have entered the field and trampled the crop. E.coli O157 is a naturally occurring organism in pigs' intestines, but it is deadly to humans," Mark said.

"So, it could have happened to anyone," Roger said. He wanted that to be on the record.

"That's correct. But the conditions at Green Earth Organic's Las Flores plant enabled the bacteria to multiply. We will issue recommendations that consumers carefully check use-by dates and avoid consuming Green Earth Organic's spinach products until we are certain they are safe again. This concludes this portion of our investigation. We will be conducting interviews with individuals in the coming months and expect to issue a final report at a later date. We will not be taking questions on this call, but will work closely with the implicated parties to resolve outstanding questions. That's all for now, thank you."

The line went dead.

"Well, that settles that. They've got their smoking gun and their scapegoat," Roger said.

Emily Putnam was packing files into boxes when Jane met her in the conference room GEO had set aside for the investigators.

"This ends the on-site inspection portion of our investigation. We still have quite a bit more analysis and interviews to perform before we issue a final report," Emily said.

"Of course. We're here if you need anything. We are as eager to conclude this investigation as you are," Jane said.

"I'm sure you are," Emily said. "We'll be in touch."

Jane watched as they pulled out of the parking lot and drove north toward to airport. Relieved to have the investigators finally gone, she returned to her desk and opened her inbox.

"Let the lawsuits begin," she said to herself.

> From: James Bogey
> Sent: Friday, September 12, 2008, 10:14 a.m.
> To: Roger Worthington, Jane Janhusen
> Subject: you may want to read this…
>
> *Brian Joseph Malmquist, "Our Little Buddy"*
> *08/01/06–09/8/08*
> *Tipton, Iowa*
>
> *Brian Joseph Malmquist, age two, passed away Monday, September 8, 2008, in Cedar Rapids, Iowa, following complications associated with hemolytic-uremic syndrome. Brian graced us with his birth August 1, 2006, where he was born at his family home in Tipton. He was the son of Scott Peter Malmquist and Ruth Anne Garvey Malmquist.*
>
> *"Our little angel will continue to live in our hearts through loving memory. He delighted in playing with his brothers, kissing his baby sister, and being read to. Above all, he enjoyed singing his Raffi songs loudly and spreading joy to all who knew him," said Brian's father, Scott Malmquist.*

> *Brian is survived by his two older brothers, Bucky and*
> *Brady; his sister, Brianna; and his grandparents, Bill and Karen*
> *Malmquist and Leif and Margaret Garvey of Tipton. Funeral*
> *services will be held at 11:00 a.m. on Thursday, September 11,*
> *2008, at the LDS Tipton Center, 2817 Mills Road in Tipton*
> *where friends may visit September 10 from 6:30–8:30 p.m. or*
> *September 11, from 9:30–10:30 a.m. Graveside services will be*
> *held Thursday at 4:00 p.m. at the Gate of Heaven Cemetery,*
> *4576 East Riverside Drive, Bennett, Iowa, under the direction*
> *of Stafford Brothers Mortuary.*
>
> *An online guest book can be found at www.staffordmortuary.*
> *com. Donations to the charity set up in his honor, Brian's Project,*
> *may be made by contacting info@briansproject.org.*

A toddler. Shit. This would be a whole new twist in the public relations strategy. She forwarded the e-mail to Roger and then picked up her phone to call Caroline.

"Caroline, it's Jane. Can you look up Brian's Project in Tipton, Iowa? I have an idea of who to invite to our employee meeting."

As soon as she hung up with Caroline, she dialed Roger.

"Did you see Bogey's e-mail? How should I respond?" Jane asked.

"You shouldn't. Let our insurance company attorneys talk to him. He's just laying the groundwork for his settlement demand letters. He's trying to intimidate us with unsubstantiated claims. There's no proof the kid ate our spinach."

"I'll ignore it. But I'm thinking of reaching out to the mother. She's started a food safety awareness organization in Brian's honor, and I'm thinking GEO could support it."

"Run it by the attorneys first."

"We won't mention specific cases, just that GEO wants to be supportive of food safety awareness. Generates goodwill. We need it. What are the latest sales numbers?"

"We're down fifty percent, but I think we've plateaued. Looks like our numbers started going back up again yesterday. Consumers have a short attention span for these things. Any word from Stella on our offer?"

"You mean your offer. Nothing yet. Her shift starts at four."

"I'd like to meet with her when she gets here. Let's get this settled before Kate returns. Her flight lands at six o'clock tonight."

CHAPTER 41

When Stella reported for her shift at 4 p.m., Jane was waiting for her in the smock room.

"Roger would like to meet with you. Tell your supervisor we're working on the employee meeting presentation," Jane said.

Stella hung her jacket on a hook and left her bump cap in her cubby. Her meeting with the police had left her feeling stronger and more confident. Roger's offer was irrelevant now. Still, she liked the feeling of holding a full house close to her chest.

Roger greeted them with a smile and motioned for them to sit down.

"Please, have a seat. Have you had a chance to consider my offer, Stella?"

"Yes."

"That's great. I think you'll be happy, and you'll never have to deal with Jimmy again. You have my word."

"I don't want your money."

"Excuse me?"

Roger looked at Jane as if he hadn't heard Stella correctly.

"I said, 'I don't want your money.'"

"I'm not sure you understand, Stella. I'm offering you a home worth a hundred thousand dollars and an additional ten thousand dollars to do with what you like. That's a lot of money. You could use it to take a vacation or have that birthmark removed, whatever you like. Is there a problem with the offer?"

Stella sat with her back straight, self-conscious but as confident as she felt the day Esperanza was born.

"There's no problem. I just can't accept it. Jimmy is guilty. Rape is not a business transaction. I feel degraded and don't want to accept money for that."

Roger began to get agitated but maintained his notorious calm tone. He spoke deliberately and with his usual confidence.

"Stella, let me be clear. This is an offer you won't get again. Jimmy will not bother you again."

"That's not the point. I mean, I am scared of him, but he could do this to another woman. I can't contribute to that, even if it would mean a lot of money. I will not profit from this."

Jane looked uncomfortable.

"Jane, tell Stella what a mistake she's making here. This is a bigger issue than Jimmy. GEO's had enough bad press in recent days. We don't need to add another incident to the list," he said.

"I don't feel comfortable telling her what to do," Jane said.

Clearly agitated, Roger stood and put both hands on his desk. He looked directly at Stella, who didn't budge.

"Fine. I don't have time to discuss this any longer. If you choose to pursue this we will not be able to help you, so you better be ready to be questioned by the police. And you can't assume that he will be found guilty. Jimmy can do some questionable things, but I have a hard time believing he is capable of rape."

Stella nodded.

"I understand," she said.

She stood and walked out of Roger's office, her ski overalls swishing with every step, as she reached into her pocket to stroke her wooden armadillo and smiled. *Nothing can stop me. Mi pequeño pájaro volará.*

CHAPTER 42

Jane drove directly to Santa Lucinda to meet Kate after her meeting with Roger and Stella. She would brief Kate on the status of the FDA investigation, the employee meeting, listen to Kate tell her about the Euclid, and then call it a week. Or had it been two weeks? She couldn't remember her last day off. She wanted to get home, curl up with her cat, and eat a pint of Baskin Robbins chocolate mint ice cream.

Kate was waiting for her when she opened the marketing office door.

"Jane! How are you? We have so much to discuss!"

"You're a refreshing sight. You look better than the rest of us. It's been a bruising two weeks to say the least." Jane put down several file boxes she was carrying. The circles under her eyes were darker than normal, and her skin looked pale. Kate had never seen her looking so disheveled before.

"You must be exhausted. Let's talk in my office. I only have an hour before I'm supposed to meet Roger for dinner. We're going to his favorite place, the Paloma Grill."

"Right, he loves that place."

Kate was as energized as Jane had ever seen her. It was as if the outbreak was happening to another company. Before Jane could even put her laptop case down and carry the file boxes in, Kate was talking nonstop.

"Aurora was great. You were right. At first I didn't like what she had to say, but by the time I left, I understood. She was brutally honest with me, Jane."

"What did she say?"

"Well, first of all she was very tuned in to my disconnects."

"Your disconnects? What does that mean?"

"You know: my love of the earth and the fact that we use so much plastic packaging. She says it's causing me anxiety and stopping me from achieving my true goals, which include being in harmony with the earth and a leader in the sustainable food movement."

Jane nodded and listened as Kate talked for another twenty minutes.

"It's all about innovation. Roger and I have to lead the way on new packaging solutions that don't pollute the oceans and seep toxins into soil and waterways."

"I think there's a lot of potential there, Kate. I like it."

"Enough about me. Fill me in on the outbreak. Where are we in the investigation? Have there been any more reports of illness? Deaths?"

Jane handed her the FDA press release and Brian Malmquist's obituary.

"The obit is courtesy of James Bogey. Word is the family has declined his offer to represent them. Religious beliefs or something like that. We're cooperating with the FDA and have hired one of the top epidemiologists in the country to help us prepare for lawsuits. No doubt, this is the first of many e-mails from Bogey. He's contacting all the victims families about suing us."

Kate read the release, her enthusiasm abruptly dampened.

"How many cases do you think there will be?"

"Hard to say. Hundreds probably. It's going to be a while before this is behind us. I'm thinking of reaching out to Brian Malmquist's mother. They've started a nonprofit in his memory. Its mission is to raise awareness about food safety. I think we may be able to support them in a way that's beneficial for both of us."

"Well, as Roger always says: 'At the end of the day, you have to be agile and adjust to the current situation.' Right? Food safety is our new battle cry."

"Right. Speaking of Roger, I hear he's got your favorite table reserved at the Paloma Grill. You better get going."

Jane stood to give Kate a hug.

"I'm glad you got some time away, Kate. But it's good to have you back."

CHAPTER 43

Monday, September 15, 2008

On Monday the news channels were abuzz with the New York Stock Exchange collapse. It was as if the world as everyone knew it was coming to an end. Jane watched CNN as she put on her makeup.

How could so much have changed in twelve days? What was the next shoe to drop? At least GEO wasn't going bankrupt, not yet anyway. She watched as Lehman Brothers employees walked out of their building in Manhattan, carrying boxes filled with their personal belongings. Cubicles, some of them inhabited for years, were cleaned out within hours. *They look even more shell-shocked than we have in recent days.*

She went straight to her Las Flores office, eager to meet with Roger and resolve the Stella issue as quickly as possible. She would advise Roger to fire Jimmy ASAP. It would be up to Stella to press charges. After pouring herself a cup of coffee, she sat at her desk and opened her e-mail. The first one to appear was from Mike Millies.

From: Mike Millies
Sent: Monday, September 15, 2008, 7:48 a.m.
To: Roger Worthington
cc: Jane Janhusen
Subject: GEO acquisition talks

Roger,

Thanks for dinner the other night. It was our pleasure to learn more about Green Earth Organics and meet your team. We've discussed internally your interest in pursuing a sale of the company and have been watching news reports on the outbreak. It appears to be settling down a bit, and we commend you for navigating through such a difficult time for your company. We are hopeful GEO will survive and thrive. However, due to the volatility in the markets and recent news regarding Lehman Brothers, we have decided to hold off on all pending transaction negotiations at this time. We look forward to resuming talks once your legal issues are resolved and we have gained more confidence in the fresh produce space.

Sincerely,
Mike Millies, Partner
Summit Capital

She dialed Roger's extension but was put through to voicemail.

"Roger, it's Jane. Call me when you get in. Thanks. Oh, and by the way, I saw Mike Millies's e-mail. You wouldn't want those vultures at Summit Capital swooping down on GEO anyway. Bye."

She hung up and called Caroline next.

"Caroline, it's Jane. I'd like to talk about the employee meeting. I've made some changes on the speaker lineup. I also have an update on the Las Flores Women's Shelter donation. We're ready to donate ten thousand dollars. Let's talk when you get in."

She stood and moved her desk chair back before stretching her arms toward the ceiling and assuming a stranding tree yoga pose. She closed her eyes, took a deep breath in, and held it. Her phone buzzed before she exhaled.

"Jane. It's the front desk. The Las Flores police are here. They're asking for Jimmy Migliozzi."

Within ten minutes Jimmy had been summoned from the wash lines and was standing in the reception area of GEO's main office building. Jane greeted the police officers at the front desk.

"Is there something we can assist you with?" she asked.

"No, Ma'am," the officer said. "We'd just like to take Mr. Migliozzi down to the station to ask him a few questions."

"May I ask what this is in regards to?"

"Criminal complaint. Filed against him last week. Evidence backs up that he may have been involved."

Jimmy was not resisting. He looked more embarrassed than anything. "Sure thing, Officer. Let me just get my jacket, and I'll meet you back here."

"That won't be necessary. We just need you to get in the back of the car, and we'll head downtown. Shouldn't take too long."

Jimmy looked at Jane and laughed uncomfortably.

"Whatever you say. You've got the gun," Jimmy said.

The officers led him to the car without incident, pushing his head down as he climbed in to the backseat and shut the door.

Jane turned to the receptionist and gave her a shrug.

"Never a dull moment, eh?"

Good for Stella. Good for her.

CHAPTER 44

Two weeks later—October 1, 2008
Tipton, Iowa

Ruth was making butter and jelly sandwiches for Bucky and Brady when the phone rang. The screen showed an 831 area code she didn't recognize. She juggled Brianna on one hip and wiped her hand on a towel before picking up the receiver.

"Hello?"

"Hi. This is Jane Janhusen from Green Earth Organics. I'm calling for Ruth Malmquist."

Ruth's heart skipped a beat at the sound of her voice.

"This is Ruth."

"Hi, Ruth. I'm calling to talk about Brian's Project. Green Earth Organics would like to donate. We'd like to invite you to receive a check at our annual employee meeting on October fifteenth."

The meeting, Jane continued, would be an "educational roundtable" on GEO's new food safety program, Clean and Clear, and showcase the importance of testing for pathogens.

"Our industry-leading food safety practices are going to shift thinking about food safety and produce. We want to share what we've learned and help promote Brian's Project with a substantial donation. We're hoping other companies adopt our testing program to make the whole industry safer."

Ruth was silent. She saw Brian's face covered in an oxygen mask and surrounded by tubes. Then his tiny body dressed in a white suit and laid in the casket. Jane waited for her to respond. She could hear children in the background, and Brianna tugging on the phone cord.

"Are you with the same Green Earth Organics that killed my son?"

Jane took a deep breath and paused before answering. Ruth waited quietly on the other end for a response.

"Yes. I'm very sorry for your loss. We are doing everything we can to cooperate with investigators to prevent another incident, which is why I am reaching out to support Brian's Project."

"Well, I appreciate that but I'll need to talk to my husband first. It's still very painful for us to talk about. We just buried Brian two weeks ago."

"I understand. We want to honor Brian's memory."

"Do you? Or is this some sort of publicity stunt to get your sales back up?"

"Not at all. We are genuinely concerned about food safety and trying to do the right thing. We're working with the top scientists in the country to establish state-of-the-art pathogen testing methods. I would love to partner with Brian's Project to talk about how we can educate the public on food safety and prevent another tragedy like this from happening again. I hope you will consider it."

"As I said, I'll have to think about it and talk it over with my husband," Ruth said.

"Of course," Jane said. "I understand. We'll wait to hear back from you."

Scott and Ruth discussed Jane's offer that night over homemade lasagna. Since Brian's funeral, they had been spending quiet time at home, nursing Bucky back to health and trying to regain some normalcy.

"Absolutely you should go," Scott said. "How much are they going to donate?"

"She didn't say, except that it would be 'substantial.' What about Bucky? He needs me here now."

"Ruthie, think of Brian. Your mom and I can take care of Bucky and Brady. You can take Brianna with you. This is for Brian's Project. Funding will help us prevent this from happening to another family."

Ruth cleared the dishes as Scott read *Busiest Fire Fighters Ever* to Bucky and Brady. Brianna was happily kicking a floor mobile on the floor beside them.

This is for you, Brian. I miss you so much. I'm going to do this for you.

"You're right, sweetie. I'll call her back tomorrow and let her know I'll be there."

CHAPTER 45

Las Flores, California
October 15, 2008

Employees mingled around picnic tables set up to seat nine hundred people in the parking lot of the Las Flores plant. The annual meeting, normally a festive affair, was clouded with anxiety. Rumors of layoffs and downsizing had been circulating since September 4. Production runs were barely getting back to normal as sales slowly crept up toward pre-outbreak targets.

The E. coli outbreak had hit the company like a tsunami, leaving massive damage. Morale was low, and management was tight-lipped and nervous about their own jobs as people compared stories they saw on the news and read online. Smoky barbecue chicken aromas filled the air as employees awaited the start of the program. Everyone was eager to hear the "State of GEO" address.

On the stage, a huge screen acted as a backdrop for a podium and several chairs. Jane wanted to showcase that GEO was alive and well. Her team was hard at work running around to make sure the caterer had enough plates for lunch and the microphones worked properly. It had been six weeks since the FDA called with news of a possible E. coli outbreak, and she was determined to prove that they had made it though the worst of it.

Ruth stood to the side of the stage, bouncing Brianna on her hip. There were four chairs arranged in a line next to the podium, each marked with a name: Roger, Kate, Ruth, and Stella.

Before she stood to speak, Ruth turned to Stella and asked if she would hold Brianna. Brianna's wide blue eyes stared at Stella as she gently bounced her on one knee. Colorful Malmquist family snapshots dominated the eight-foot-tall screen behind Ruth as she spoke.

"My son's life will be remembered through Brian's Project, a nonprofit advocacy group my husband, Scott, and I have started to raise awareness about food safety. We will collaborate with consumer groups, Congress, and companies like Green Earth Organics to encourage other companies to test for pathogens and prevent a similar tragedy from happening to another family."

Employees applauded as Kate stood and presented Ruth with an oversize check for $200,000 made out to Brian's Project. A photographer was standing nearby to capture the moment. Kate looked right at him, smiling. She hugged Ruth before stepping up to the podium herself.

"Thank you, Ruth, for coming here today and sharing your story with us. Green Earth Organics is committed to working with Brian's Project to advance our testing program and set the gold standard for pathogen testing in the fresh-cut produce industry."

Employees applauded again as Kate thanked the crowd.

"Next we'll hear from longtime GEO employee Stella Gonzalez on our new Clean and Clear program, a state-of-the art solution to some of the biggest challenges facing the fresh-cut produce industry."

Stella stood and took a deep breath before stepping up to the podium. She guided the crowd through a series of slides illustrating the steps of the testing program.

"Hello. My name is Stella Gonzalez, and I have worked at GEO since 1992."

She took a deep breath and looked out at the hundreds of GEO employees seated in chairs and standing in front of the stage. Her heart raced and she looked at Jane, sitting in the front row. Jane nodded and smiled, giving her two thumbs-up and mouthed, "You can do it!"

Stella shifted her weight from foot to foot and continued.

"I'm here today to share with you what GEO is doing to make fresh produce safer. We've started a new program called Clean and Clear that will revolutionize the way bagged greens are delivered. First we randomly choose one bag of greens from every case ready to ship. Then we pull out a sample of greens and place them in a tray to be tested. Once that's done, we place the sample in a bag and label it as we wait for the test results to come back. This way, we are ensuring that all the product GEO ships is free of pathogens and lives up to our mission to enrich the earth."

Giant pictures of the lab and wash lines flashed on the screen behind her. The crowd applauded as Stella stepped down from the stage and returned to her table next to Ofelia.

"Thank you, Stella, for helping us become a pioneer in food safety!" Kate said.

Stella smiled and nodded before leaning in and whispering to Ofelia.

"See you later. I'm leaving."

"What? The one day they feed us and give us a couple of hours off and you're leaving? I don't get you."

Stella smiled at Ofelia and gave her a big hug.

"Remember how I told you I was going to leave GEO?"

"Which time? You say that every day."

"Well, I'm doing it. Today. Never coming back."

"Right, Stella! I'll see you here tomorrow."

"No. I mean it this time. I gave notice this morning. Maybe you want to quit with me, Offie?"

"Yeah, right. And do what? Someone has to pay for Bobby's beer."

"Well, you think about it. I'm going to need some help at my new company. There's only a few months left before the move. Maybe you can finish out the season, and then we'll talk."

"What's your new business? Are you and Pretty Boy starting that landscaping company you always talk about?"

"It's not a landscaping business. It's home farming, planting edible gardens for people. We're thinking more along the lines of practical maintenance and beautification. What do you think?"

"I think I need some *maintenance and beautification.*"

"Well, you know who to call!"

Stella slipped out of the employee meeting and walked to the lunchroom where she grabbed her lunch box. Emiliano was waiting for her in the parking lot, his truck engine running. She could hear Roger's bellowing voice in the background as he paced back and forth on the stage, a microphone clipped to his black mock turtleneck. A video of fieldworkers harvesting lettuce played on the screen while Kelly Clarkson's *Stronger* blared from the speakers.

"What doesn't kill you makes you stronger!"

Applause erupted from the audience.

"Green Earth Organics will emerge from this recall stronger than ever! We are developing a breakthrough testing program that will be the gold standard in the fresh-cut produce industry!" Roger said.

Emiliano stood by his truck with his hands behind his back. He grinned and moved his arm toward Stella to present her with a huge bouquet of fresh flowers. "From my home farm!" he said. Stella hugged him in delight before he opened the passenger side door for her.

"Your carriage awaits, my star."

They pulled out of the parking lot and turned left out the driveway, leaving fifteen years of work on the wash lines behind, without anyone noticing.

CHAPTER 46

Cedar Rapids, Iowa
October 16, 2008

Ruth arrived at the Eastern Iowa Airport right on time. She walked with Brianna on her hip down the arrivals terminal to find Scott waiting for her with Bucky and Brady.

"Mommy! Mommy!" Brady shouted. "We got a puppy! We got a puppy!"

Scott picked him up and put his finger over his mouth.

"Shhhh. Brady! It's supposed to be a surprise."

"A puppy, eh?" Ruth said. "Well, that's what I get for going away for a couple of days!"

She leaned down to give Bucky a kiss and asked how he was feeling.

"Better every day, Mama."

"That's my boy. Daddy kept his puppy promise, I guess."

"Yep!" Bucky said. "I wish Brian were here to play with him. He peed all over the living room!"

"Oh, great! Brian is here in spirit, sweetie. I can feel him smiling down on you."

"What should we name him?" Scott asked.

"Ryan! Let's name him Ryan after Dr. Ryan," Bucky said. "And it sounds like Brian."

"I like it," Ruth said.

"Ryan it is," Scott said, and gave Bucky a high-five.

Scott wrapped his arm around Ruth and Brianna. Bucky and Brady each clung to Scott's legs, forming a group hug. He whispered in her ear.

"Brian will always be with us."

"I know," she said. "I know."

Scott wiped a tear from her cheek. Then he picked up Brady and took Bucky's hand.

"Should we go home and introduce Mommy to Ryan?"

The boys could hardly contain themselves with excitement.

"Yes! Yes! You're going to love him, Mommy!"

"I'm sure I will, boys. I'm sure I will."

CHAPTER 47

The day after the employee meeting, Stella and Emiliano went to Las Flores High School to watch Esperanza play in a volleyball game. Raul was sitting in the stands with a group of friends when he spotted Stella and greeted her with a polite wave.

"Hey, Ms. Gonzalez."

"Hi, Raul. How are you?"

"I'm good. Esperanza tells me you might be starting your own farming business."

"That's right," Stella said. She introduced him to Emiliano, who shook his hand and gave him an approving nod.

"Why? You looking for a job?" Emiliano asked.

"Yeah, I kinda am. I'm going to work for a few years while I apply for citizenship and go to junior college. My goal is to get to Berkeley someday."

"Well, let's talk. Stella and I could use a third person. It would mean we could take on a few more clients. But you're going to have to prove that you're a hard worker and if you ever hurt Esperanza, not only will you be out of a job you'll have me to deal with."

Raul stood up straight and looked Emiliano in the eye.

"I can assure you I am a hard worker and would never hurt Esperanza, Mr. Cayeros. She's the one who would hurt me. When do I start?" He put his hand out to shake and Emiliano gave him a firm grip.

"I'll meet you at Stella's house at 6 a.m. sharp."

"See you there."

After the game, Stella invited Raul back to the house for a platter of Gran's homemade enchiladas. When the four of them walked in the kitchen, Gran was sitting at the table in her apron, watching television.

"Finally! I've been waiting all day for you. I've made enough enchiladas to feed all of Las Flores."

The five of them sat down to eat, and Esperanza pulled out a letter from her backpack.

"I've been waiting to show you this, Mama," she said. "I thought you should be the first to see it."

Stella unfolded the letter and started reading. Then she looked up at Esperanza with tears streaming down her face. "You got into Berkeley?"

"Conditional. The volleyball coach has offered me a spot on the team. As long as I keep my grades up this year, she said I'm in—with a scholarship to help cover my tuition and living expenses."

Stella screamed with joy and clasped her hands together. She reached into a kitchen cabinet where she kept their nicest dishes and took out a small package wrapped in newspaper. Inside was a painted wooden figurine of a bird, much like her armadillo.

"You did it! *Nuestro pequeño pájaro!* I have saved this for you. Your grandfather painted it and would want you to have it now."

Esperanza held the bird, bursting with bright primary colors and thousands of tiny dots.

"*Gracias*, mama. It's beautiful."

Raul hugged her next and pulled a rose from his backpack.

"For you," he said, and leaned in to give her a kiss.

"I'm only a couple of hours away, and you'll be there in two years, right?"

"Of course. And every weekend if your mom and Emiliano give me time off."

Stella held the letter as if it were a priceless artifact. She kept rereading it, bursting with joy for Esperanza, Gran, her father, and her grandparents.

"You have made us so proud, *mija*! So many people are smiling down on you right now. You will be the first Gonzalez to go to college and not have to work in the fields or in a cold box on the wash lines. Your work has made our work worth it all. Sixty years of labor is in this letter."

Esperanza hugged her mother and whispered into her ear, "I love you, Mama. Thank you for teaching me to fly."

CHAPTER 48

Las Flores, California
Six months later—April, 2009

"What do you think?" Emiliano stood back from his truck, hands resting on his hips.

A friend had designed a new decal for the doors: *Stella's Home Farming. Your source for fresh, homegrown vegetables.* The words surrounded an illustration of a colorful armadillo. Below the logo it read: "Go local. Call us today! (831) 901-2673."

"I like it," Gran said. "How do I sign up?"

Stella and Emiliano were working with more than a dozen homeowners to design, plant, and maintain home vegetable gardens. They charged twenty dollars an hour each, more than doubling the pay they had been earning on the wash line, and couldn't keep up with demand. Stella had converted a corner in the kitchen into a small office where Ofelia answered calls and kept track of invoices.

"Why did this take me so long to do?" Stella asked Emiliano as they unloaded the day's planting supplies from his truck.

"You just needed the confidence to go out on your own," he said. "It's not an easy transition."

"You're right. I wish my confidence didn't have to be sparked by Pinocchio. I don't know why I didn't get out of there sooner."

"Any word on that?"

"He's pleading guilty to avoid a trial. My attorney says he could get three years. The most important thing is he didn't get away with it. And

GEO fired him. I also heard Jane left. Supposedly she took a job with Patagonia, helping them source plastic junk from the Pacific to make their fleece jackets with."

"Really?" Emiliano asked. "That's a big change from promoting Kate and Roger all day every day."

"Yeah, they're still trying to sell the company. Gregg Fluerant tells me all the latest news every time I'm planting a new vegetable for him."

"So that's how you know everything! His home farm is huge!"

"It's not huge, but it's diverse," Stella laughed. "We're using a no-till system and planting hairy vetch and subterranean clover mulches as a cover crop. I keep telling him he should just quit GEO and sell his heirloom tomatoes at the Santa Lucinda Farmer's Market!"

"He said Roger's last three attempts to sell the company fell through at the last minute. They want out so bad they've slashed the price. They're probably going to get three hundred million dollars from some German company looking to get into organics. I'm just glad I don't have to see Pinocchio every day and worry about getting laid off."

"Don't mess with Stella Gonzalez!" Emiliano gave her a high-five and smiled at Gran.

Esperanza flew through the front door toward the three of them in a short dress and platform heels.

"You guys need to get ready! We're going to be late!" she called.

They were scheduled to be at the Las Flores High Senior Night in an hour. Esperanza was being honored for getting her volleyball scholarship to UC Berkeley.

"Sí! We'll be ready," Stella exclaimed. "We've been ready for sixty years."

Emiliano picked her up and swung her around. "Then we better get going, my shining star."

ACKNOWLEDGMENTS

This book would not have happened without the inspiration, encouragement and support of many people. First, I would like to thank the millions of people who plant, grow, harvest, process and serve the food we eat. From farmers to field workers to manufacturing plant and restaurant workers, there is a long chain of hardworking people who bring food to our tables. Often, they are invisible, low paid and underappreciated. They inspired me to tell this story.

I also want to recognize the Malmquists of the world: victims of foodborne illnesses. I can't imagine the pain of losing a child or loved one to something as simple as food we trust, and I hope this story honors their experiences in a respectful way.

A list of early readers' honest and constructive criticism made this a better story. Thank you to Jim Petkiewicz, Vicky Montoya, Maryalice Whalen, Katie Morris, Debbie Palmer, and Jean Matthias Breheney. Without your keen eyes and suggestions, my plot line and characters would still be a tangled mess. I am also grateful for the ongoing encouragement of Sara Singleton, Mary March, Deborah Wright, Heather Hafleigh, Joe Torquato, and Byron Palmer. My talented photographer friend, Elaine Patarini, graciously offered to take my author's photo before I realized I should have one.

I am fortunate to be included in a talented community of supportive writers: Stephen Pearsall and Ronne Thompson (Somers Loop Writing Group) and Kathy McKenzie and Corey Anderson (Mission City

Writers Group.) Special thanks to Devra Saxton for her informative and in depth research on farmworkers in the Central Valley of California, which I turned to for accurate details about Stella's life.

Most of all, I want to thank my family. My children, Sarah and Jack, listened to me talk about this project for a decade and never discouraged me. My patient husband, Joe, allowed me the time, space and encouragement to write this book. For all of you, I am forever grateful.

CPSIA information can be obtained
at www.ICGtesting.com
Printed in the USA
FSOW01n0305310317
32530FS